CHILDREN'S STORYBOOK BIBLE

101 BIBLE STORIES
retold especially for children

Children's Storybook Bible: 101 Bible Stories

Copyright © 2023 by International Publishing Services Pty Ltd Sydney Australia (IPS) & North Parade Publishing Ltd Bath UK (NPP) Publishers, Peter Hicks and Wayne McKay.
All rights reserved.

Illustrations copyright © IPS & NPP. All rights reserved.

Written by J Emmerson-Hicks

ISBN 978-1-83923-937-3

Printed in China

29   28 27   26 25 24 23 7   6   5   4   3   2   1

CHILDREN'S STORYBOOK BIBLE

101 BIBLE STORIES
retold especially for children

taken from the Illustrated Children's Bible

CONTENTS

THE OLD TESTAMENT

GOD MAKES THE WORLD Genesis 1–2	4
DISOBEYING GOD Genesis 3	6
NOAH BUILDS AN ARK Genesis 6–7	8
THE FLOOD Genesis 7–9	10
THE TOWER OF BABEL Genesis 11	12
A PROMISE TO ABRAHAM Genesis 12–13, 15–17	14
ABRAHAM IS TESTED Genesis 21–22	16
A WIFE FOR ISAAC Genesis 24	18
THE BOWL OF STEW Genesis 25–27	20
JACOB'S DREAM Genesis 28	22
TWELVE BROTHERS Genesis 37	24
BROTHER FOR SALE Genesis 37	26
THROWN INTO JAIL Genesis 39–40	28
PHARAOH'S DREAMS Genesis 41	30
REUNITED Genesis 41–47	32
A BABY IN THE REEDS Exodus 1–2	34
PHARAOH SAYS NO! Exodus 3–7	36
THE TEN PLAGUES Exodus 7–12	38
CROSSING THE RED SEA Exodus 12–15	40
FOOD AND WATER IN THE DESERT Exodus 15–17	42
THE TEN COMMANDMENTS Exodus 19–20	44
THE GOLDEN CALF Exodus 32	46
THE TWELVE SPIES Numbers 13–14	48
WATER FROM A ROCK Numbers 20	50
JOSHUA TAKES COMMAND Deuteronomy 31–34	52
THE WALLS OF JERICHO Joshua 3–4, 6	54
THE SUN AND THE MOON Joshua 10	56
GIDEON AND THE THREE HUNDRED Judges 6–7	58
SAMSON THE STRONG Judges 13, 16	60
FAITHFUL RUTH Ruth 1–4	62
HANNAH'S PRAYER 1 Samuel 1–2	64
THE SHEPHERD BOY 1 Samuel 16–17	66
THE WISDOM OF SOLOMON 1 Kings 3; 2 Chronicles 1	68
GOD'S TEMPLE 1 Kings 5–8; 2 Chronicles 2–7	70
ELIJAH AND THE RAVENS 1 Kings 17	72
THE GREAT CONTEST 1 Kings 18	74
TAKEN TO HEAVEN 2 Kings 2	76
WASHED CLEAN 2 Kings 5	78
JEHOSHAPHAT TRUSTS GOD 2 Chronicles 20	80
HEZEKIAH'S PRAYER 2 Kings 18–19; 2 Chronicles 32	82
THE POTTER'S CLAY Jeremiah 1, 18–20	84
THE FALL OF JERUSALEM Jeremiah 29; 2 Chronicles 36; Isaiah 40	86
THE FIERY FURNACE Daniel 3	88
DANIEL IN THE LIONS' DEN Daniel 6	90
RETURN TO JERUSALEM Ezra 1	92
REBUILDING THE WALLS Nehemiah 1–4	94
BEAUTIFUL ESTHER Esther 1–3	96
THE BRAVE QUEEN Esther 4–9	98
JONAH AND THE BIG FISH Jonah 1–2	100

THE NEW TESTAMENT

A VISIT FROM AN ANGEL Luke 1	102
BORN IN A MANGER Luke 2	104

Title	Page
THE SHEPHERDS' STORY Luke 2	106
THE BRIGHT STAR Matthew 2	108
"MY FATHER'S HOUSE" Matthew 2; Luke 2	110
JESUS IS BAPTISED Matthew 3; Mark 1; Luke 3	112
TESTED IN THE DESERT Matthew 4; Mark 1; Luke 4	114
FISHING FOR MEN Matthew 4; Mark 1; Luke 5	116
WATER INTO WINE John 2	118
"YOU CAN MAKE ME CLEAN!" Matthew 8; Mark 1; Luke 4–5	120
WHERE THERE'S A WILL... Matthew 9; Mark 2; Luke 5	122
THE WOMAN AT THE WELL John 4	124
THE OFFICER'S SERVANT Matthew 8; Luke 7	126
JUST SLEEPING Matthew 9; Luke 8	128
SERMON ON THE MOUNT Matthew 5–7; Luke 6	130
THE RIGHT WAY TO PRAY Matthew 6–7; Luke 11	132
A FIRM FOUNDATION Matthew 7; Luke 6	134
JESUS CALMS THE STORM Matthew 8; Mark 4; Luke 8	136
PARABLE OF THE SOWER Matthew 13; Mark 4; Luke 8	138
PARABLE OF THE WEEDS Matthew 13	140
THE BIG PICNIC Matthew 14; Mark 6; Luke 9; John 6	142
WALKING ON WATER Matthew 14; Mark 6; John 6	144
JESUS AND THE CHILDREN Matthew 19; Mark 10; Luke 18	146
THE GOOD SAMARITAN Luke 10	148
THE LOST SON Luke 15	150
MARTHA AND MARY Luke 10; John 11	152
THE RICH RULER Matthew 19; Mark 10; Luke 18	154
BE READY! Matthew 24–25; Mark 13; Luke 21; John 12	156
ZACCHAEUS IN THE TREE Luke 19	158
LOST AND FOUND Matthew 18; Luke 15; John 10	160
THE EXPENSIVE PERFUME Matthew 26; Mark 14; John 12	162
JESUS ENTERS JERUSALEM Matthew 21; Mark 11; Luke 19; John 12	164
TROUBLE IN THE TEMPLE Matthew 21; Mark 11; Luke 19	166
THE WIDOW'S OFFERING Mark 12; Luke 21	168
LIKE A SERVANT John 13	170
THE LORD'S SUPPER Matthew 26; Mark 14; Luke 22; John 13–15	172
A DARK NIGHT Matthew 26; Mark 14; Luke 22; John 17–18	174
PILATE WASHES HIS HANDS Matthew 27; Mark 15; Luke 23; John 18	176
THE CRUCIFIXION Matthew 27; Mark 15; Luke 23; John 19	178
ALIVE! Matthew 28; Mark 16; Luke 24; John 20	180
A STRANGER ON THE ROAD Mark 16; Luke 24	182
DOUBTING THOMAS Luke 24; John 20	184
THE ASCENSION Mark 16; Luke 24; Acts 1	186
THE HOLY SPIRIT Acts 2	188
TROUBLE! Acts 3–5	190
PHILIP AND THE ETHIOPIAN Acts 8	192
SAUL SEES THE LIGHT Acts 9	194
THE SHEET OF ANIMALS Acts 10	196
SINGING IN PRISON Acts 16	198
STORM AT SEA Acts 27–28	200
THE GREATEST OF THESE Romans 8, 12; 1 Corinthians 12–13	202
"I'M COMING SOON!" Revelation	204

THE OLD TESTAMENT

GOD MAKES THE WORLD

In the beginning, there was nothing at all. Then God created the heaven and the earth, but everything was still covered in darkness, so God said, "Let there be light," and there was light! God called the light day and the darkness night and that was the first day and the first night!

In the days that followed, God separated the water from dry land, and covered the land with beautiful plants and trees. He made the sun to shine during the day and the moon and stars to light up the night sky.

Then God filled the seas with enormous whales and shiny fish, leaping dolphins and wobbly jellyfish, and he filled the skies with colourful birds. He made animals of all shapes and sizes – swift cheetahs, slow tortoises, huge elephants, and many more.

Last of all, God made man and told him to take care of this wonderful world and all the creatures.

God was pleased with all he had made and done, so on the seventh day, he rested, and made that day a special day to rest and give thanks.

God told Adam that he might help himself to fruit from any of the trees except for one: the Tree of Knowledge. He brought the animals and birds to Adam so that he could name them. But none of the animals were like him, and Adam was lonely, so God created a woman, Eve, to be his special friend. God loved Adam and Eve and gave them everything they needed.

DISOBEYING GOD

Now, of all the animals, the most cunning was the snake. One day, he said to Eve, "Did God really tell you that you couldn't eat fruit from any of the trees in this garden?" and she replied, "Oh no, we can eat from any of them except from the one in the middle of the garden!"

"The Tree of Knowledge?" asked the wily snake. "But the fruit is delicious and it won't harm you in the slightest! The only reason God doesn't want you to eat it is because it will make you wise like him. Go on, take a bite!"

The fruit looked so delicious that Eve picked some. She offered some to Adam, too, and they both ate it.

At once, it was as though their eyes had been opened. They realised they were naked and tried to cover themselves with some fig leaves.

Later that day, God was walking in the garden. When he found Adam and Eve hiding behind some bushes, he knew exactly what had happened. He was very angry. He cursed the wicked snake to crawl on its belly in the dirt for the rest of its life, and he banished Adam and Eve from the Garden of Eden. He told them that from now on they would need to work hard to get their food from the ground, and would have to struggle with sharp thorns and choking weeds, for they had disobeyed him.

Then he used some animal skins to make clothes for them, and sent them away from the beautiful garden. He placed an angel with a flaming sword to stand guard at the entrance.

NOAH BUILDS AN ARK

Many years passed, and soon there were lots of people in the world. But they were becoming more and more wicked and this made God very sad. He made up his mind to send a terrible flood to destroy everything that he had created.

But there was one good man who loved and obeyed God. His name was Noah and he had three sons. God told Noah to build an enormous boat, an ark, so that he and his family might be saved, along with two of every living creature.

When people saw Noah building a boat in the middle of the land they laughed at him and made fun of him. But Noah ignored them, for he trusted God.

Noah built the amazing boat out of cypress wood. It had lots of rooms inside it and was three decks high! God told him exactly how it should be made and how big it should be. It took Noah and his three sons a long, long time to finish it.

When the ark was finished, Noah, his wife, and his sons and their wives loaded it with food for themselves and the animals. Then God sent the animals to the ark, two by two, one male and one female of every kind of animal that lived upon the earth or flew in the skies.

Once they were all safely in, God closed the door behind them.

THE FLOOD

As soon as Noah and his family and the animals were all safely in, it began to rain. And how it rained! Water poured down from the skies and covered all the land. Every living creature was drowned. All the towns and cities were washed away. But the ark and its precious cargo floated free on a world of water.

For forty days and forty nights it rained. Then, at last, it stopped. After a while, the flood waters began to go down. Noah sent out a dove and when it returned with an olive leaf in its beak, Noah knew that the flood was over, for the trees were growing again.

Then it was time for Noah and the animals to leave the ark. Noah was filled with gratitude and God promised him that he would never again send such a dreadful flood. He put a beautiful rainbow in the sky to remind him of this promise.

THE TOWER OF BABEL

To begin with, the whole world had only one language, so everyone could understand everyone else. But then there came a time when a group of Noah's descendants decided to settle down and build a city which would be famous throughout the land, with a magnificent tower that would reach to the heavens.

But when God saw what they were doing, he was not happy. He knew that they were becoming too proud and vain – they had forgotten about God.

So God made them unable to understand one another. Soon a great babble of voices was heard all over the city, with everyone speaking in a different language. No one could understand his neighbour.

In all the confusion, building stopped. The wonderful tower was left unfinished, the people scattered far and wide, and the tower became known as the Tower of Babel.

A PROMISE TO ABRAHAM

There was once a man called Abraham. Abraham was a good man, who trusted in God. God asked him to leave his home and go to another land. He promised to bless him and make him the father of a great nation. Abraham had a good home, but when God told him to leave, he did. He took his wife, Sarah, his nephew Lot, and his servants, and they all set out for Canaan.

Many years passed, and although Abraham became wealthy, he and his wife had no child. Yet Abraham wasn't worried – he trusted God.

God spoke to Abraham. He told him he would have too many descendants to count – as many as the stars in the sky! – and that all this land would belong to them. Then God told him to prepare a sacrifice.

That evening, God spoke to him again, telling him that his descendants would be slaves in a country not their own for four hundred years. But they would at last be free and would return to their own land, and those who had enslaved them would be punished.

When the sun had set and darkness had fallen, a smoking firepot with a blazing torch appeared and passed between the pieces of the sacrifice as a sign to Abraham from God.

ABRAHAM IS TESTED

When Sarah was ninety years old, a miracle happened – she gave birth to a baby boy, Isaac, just as God had promised! Isaac grew up to be a fine young boy and his father and mother were very proud of him, and thankful to God. But one day, God decided to test Abraham's faith. He told Abraham that he must offer the boy as a sacrifice!

Abraham was heartbroken, but his faith in God was absolute, and so he prepared everything, just as he had been commanded.

But as he lifted up his knife, an angel spoke to him, "Abraham, Abraham! Do not harm the boy! I know now that you love the Lord your God with all your heart, for you would be willing to give up your own son."

God sent a ram to be sacrificed in the boy's place, and the angel told Abraham that God would truly bless him and his descendants because of his faith.

A WIFE FOR ISAAC

When Isaac had grown into a young man, Abraham asked his most trusted servant to go back to his homeland and find a wife there for his son. This was a difficult task, and when the servant reached his master's home town, he prayed to God to send him a sign: "Let Isaac's wife be whoever comes to offer water not just to me, but to my camels also."

Before he had finished praying, beautiful Rebecca came out to draw water from the well. When the servant asked her if he might have a drink, she offered him her jar straight away, and then hurried to draw water for his camels too.

The servant thanked God for listening to his prayers. He then explained his mission to Rebecca, and when her father was asked, it was agreed that she should become Isaac's wife.

When Rebecca travelled back to Canaan to meet her new husband, Isaac fell in love with her instantly, and she with him!

THE BOWL OF STEW

Rebecca was old before she became pregnant, and when she did, it was with twins. They seemed to kick and push so much inside her that she was worried, but God told her that the two boys would one day be the fathers of two nations. The first-born was a hairy boy, whom they named Esau, and his brother was called Jacob. When they grew up, Esau became a great hunter, while Jacob was quieter and spent more time at home. Isaac loved Esau, but Rebecca was especially fond of Jacob.

One day, Jacob was preparing a delicious stew when his brother came in, ravenous after a long trip. When he demanded some of the stew, Jacob told him that he could only have some in exchange for his birthright as the first-born son. Esau was so hungry and impatient that he agreed! He had shown how little he cared about his rights as the first-born son if he was prepared to sell them for a simple meal!

When Isaac was very old and nearly blind, he wished to give his blessing to his eldest son. But Rebecca wanted her favourite son, Jacob, to receive the blessing. She helped Jacob to disguise himself as Esau, wrapping goatskins around his arms so that he would be hairy like his brother when he went in to see his father.

Jacob didn't sound like his brother, but he felt like him, and so Isaac gave him his blessing to be in charge of the family when he died.

When Esau found out what had happened, he was so angry he wanted to kill his brother! Rebecca sent Jacob away from home to keep him safe.

JACOB'S DREAM

Jacob travelled to the house of his uncle Laban. On the way, he stopped for the night. Using a hard stone as a pillow, he lay down to sleep. That night he had a dream in which he saw a stairway resting on the earth, with its top reaching to heaven, and angels were walking up and down it.

At the very top stood the Lord, and he said, "I am the Lord, the God of Abraham and of Isaac. I will give you and your descendants the land on which you lie. Your descendants will be like the dust of the earth, and you will

spread to the west and the east, to the north and the south. I am with you, and will watch over you wherever you go, and I will bring you back to this land. I will not leave you until I have done what I have promised."

TWELVE BROTHERS

Jacob lived in Canaan. He had twelve sons, but Joseph was his favourite, for he was the first son of Rachel, whom Jacob had loved dearly. To show Joseph just how much he loved him, Jacob had a wonderful coat made for him, a long-sleeved robe covered with colourful embroidery.

His brothers were jealous, but what really angered them was when he began telling them of the dreams he'd had: "Last night I dreamt we were collecting sheaves of grain, when suddenly my sheaf stood up straight and yours all bowed down before it."

"What are you saying?" growled the brothers. "You think you're going to rule over us some day? Be off with you!"

Joseph had another dream. "This time, the sun and moon and eleven stars were bowing down to me," he told his family. Even Jacob became quite cross when he heard about Joseph's latest dream. "Do you really believe that your mother and I, and all your brothers are going to bow down before you? Don't get too big for your boots!" But Jacob did wonder to himself what the dream might mean.

BROTHER FOR SALE

Joseph's brothers had had enough. They felt the time had come to get rid of their annoying brother. One day, out in the fields, they said to one another, "Here comes the dreamer! Let's kill him now and throw his body into a well!" Reuben persuaded them not to kill Joseph, but to throw him in the well without hurting him. He secretly intended to save him later.

The jealous brothers set upon young Joseph. They tore off his multi-coloured coat and threw him in a deep pit. Then they sat down nearby to eat, deaf to his cries for help.

Just then, they saw a caravan of Ishmaelite traders passing by on their way to Egypt. Quick as a flash, they decided to sell Joseph to them. It would be far more profitable than killing him! So off to Egypt went Joseph in chains, sold for twenty pieces of silver!

Then the brothers took his beautiful coat, ripped it into pieces and smeared it with the blood of a goat. Afterwards, they trooped home with long faces and showed the coat to their father, implying that Joseph had been killed by a wild animal. Poor Jacob was heartbroken at the death of his beloved son.

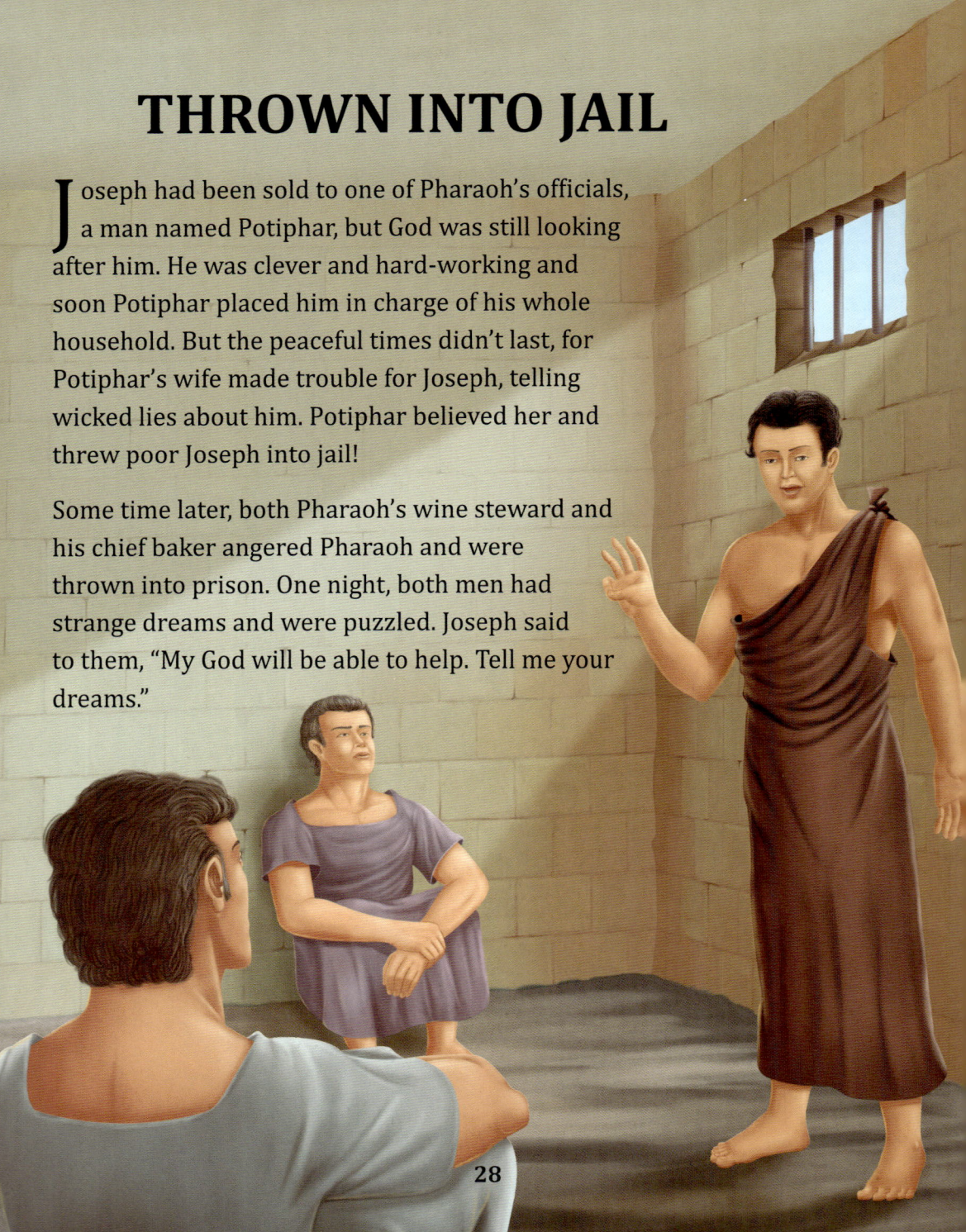

THROWN INTO JAIL

Joseph had been sold to one of Pharaoh's officials, a man named Potiphar, but God was still looking after him. He was clever and hard-working and soon Potiphar placed him in charge of his whole household. But the peaceful times didn't last, for Potiphar's wife made trouble for Joseph, telling wicked lies about him. Potiphar believed her and threw poor Joseph into jail!

Some time later, both Pharaoh's wine steward and his chief baker angered Pharaoh and were thrown into prison. One night, both men had strange dreams and were puzzled. Joseph said to them, "My God will be able to help. Tell me your dreams."

The wine steward went first: "In my dream I saw a vine, with three branches covered in grapes. I took the grapes and squeezed them into Pharaoh's cup."

Joseph told him that within three days, Pharaoh would pardon him and take him back – and he asked the steward to remember him.

Now the baker was anxious to tell his dream, too. "On my head were three baskets of bread," he said, "but birds were eating Pharaoh's pastries."

Joseph was sad. "Within three days, Pharaoh will cut off your head, and the birds will eat your flesh."

Things turned out just as Joseph foretold, for in three days it was Pharaoh's birthday, and on that day he pardoned the wine steward and gave him back his job, but he hanged the chief baker and ordered his guards to cut off his head.

PHARAOH'S DREAMS

Two long years passed, then, one night, Pharaoh had a strange dream. He was standing by the Nile when out of the river came seven cows, healthy and fat, and they grazed among the reeds. After them, seven other cows, ugly and thin, came up out of the Nile and stood beside them. Then the thin cows ate the fat cows and yet looked as thin and sickly as before!

Pharaoh had another dream. Seven healthy heads of grain were growing on a single stalk. Then seven more heads of grain sprouted, and these were thin and scorched by the wind. The thin heads of grain swallowed up the seven healthy, full heads.

In the morning, Pharaoh felt worried. None of his magicians or wise men could interpret the dreams, but then the wine bearer remembered Joseph.

The slave was brought before Pharaoh, who asked him to explain his dream. "I cannot do it," Joseph replied. "But God will be able to explain."

Once Pharaoh had told his dream, Joseph replied, "These two dreams are really one and the same. The seven cows and the seven heads of grain are seven years. The land will be blessed with seven years of healthy crops and bountiful harvests, but they will be followed by seven years of dreadful famine. You will need to plan carefully to prepare for what lies ahead."

Pharaoh spoke to his advisors, then turned to Joseph, saying, "It is clear to me that you are the man we need. Since God has made all this known to you, I will put you in charge of my land. You will be second only to me in all of Egypt."

In this way, Joseph was placed in charge of planning for the famine for all Egypt, and became a powerful man.

REUNITED!

Joseph planned so well for the famine that when it struck, Egypt's storehouses were full of food. In fact, people from other countries travelled to Egypt to buy food, for the famine was severe everywhere else, too. Joseph's brothers were among those who came to buy grain!

When they reached Egypt, the brothers bowed down before Joseph. With his golden chain and fine clothes, they didn't recognise him, but Joseph could see his dreams becoming reality, as they begged to buy food.

Joseph wanted to see if his brothers had changed at all, and so he planned to test their honesty and loyalty. First, he insisted that they return to Egypt with their youngest brother, Benjamin, who had stayed behind with their father. Then, when they did return with Benjamin, he gave them sackloads of grain and sent them on their way – but not before planting a fine silver cup in his youngest brother's sack.

Guards brought them back to the palace where they were accused of stealing. When the silver cup was found in Benjamin's sack, the horrified brothers fell to their knees. "My Lord!" they cried, "take any one of us, but do not take Benjamin, for his father's heart would break!"

At this, Joseph knew that his brothers really had changed – any one of them would have given himself up to save Benjamin. Crying tears of joy, Joseph went to hug them, and to their amazement told them who he really was. He told them not to feel too bad about what had happened, for it had all been part of God's plan. "I was sent to rule in Egypt so that you would not starve in Canaan!" he said.

The brothers were filled with joy, for they had spent many years feeling sorry for what they had done. Now, Joseph sent for Jacob and all his family to join him in Egypt where they were well treated and given good land. Joseph wept tears of happiness when his father arrived, and Jacob was overflowing with gratitude to be reunited with his beloved son.

A BABY IN THE REEDS

Long years had passed since the time of Joseph. Now there were many Hebrews in Egypt. The new Pharaoh feared they would become too strong and so he turned them into slaves. Yet still their numbers grew. Pharaoh ordered that any boys born to the Hebrews must be killed!

Moses was a beautiful baby boy. His mother loved him dearly, but knew that if the king found out about him, he would be killed. She made a basket out of bulrushes and placed him in it tenderly, then lowered him into the water among the reeds.

After a while, the king's daughter came down to the river. She heard a strange gurgling noise, and pulled back the reeds to see a lovely baby boy crying. She picked him up and held him gently in her arms. "This must be one of the Hebrew babies," she said softly.

Moses' sister Miriam was secretly watching from nearby. Now she bravely stepped forward and offered to fetch someone to nurse the baby. When the princess nodded, Miriam darted off to find her own mother, and so it was that Miriam's mother looked after her own son, until he was old enough for the princess to take him to the palace.

PHARAOH SAYS NO!

When Moses grew up, he was angry to see how the Egyptians treated his fellow Hebrews. He left Egypt and became a shepherd. One day, while Moses was tending his sheep, he noticed that a nearby bush was on fire, yet the leaves of the bush were not burning! As he stepped closer, God spoke to him and said, "I have come to rescue my people and bring them out of Egypt and into the Promised Land. You must go to Pharaoh and demand that he free them."

Moses was scared, but God would not listen to his excuses. He told Moses that he would be with him and that he would perform many miracles. He sent him back to Egypt, but he also sent Moses' brother Aaron to help him.

Moses and Aaron came before Pharaoh and said, "The God of Israel asks that you let his people go so that they may hold a festival to him in the desert." Pharaoh could not believe their nerve. "Who is this God of Israel? I don't know him and I will not let the Hebrews go!" He was so angry that he made the slaves work even harder.

So Moses and Aaron went back to Pharaoh, who demanded some proof of their god. This time, Aaron threw down his staff on the ground and it instantly was transformed into a fearsome snake. But the king's magicians huddled together and performed sorcery, and when they threw their staffs on the ground, they too turned into snakes, and even though Aaron's snake swallowed them all up, the king's heart was hardened, and he would not let the Hebrews go.

THE TEN PLAGUES

Then the Lord sent a series of plagues upon the Egyptians, each more terrible than the last. First, he changed the waters of the Nile into blood, so that all the fish died and the air stank. He sent a plague of frogs to cover the countryside and fill the houses. Next, the very dust on the ground was turned into gnats, and everything was covered with them. After them, came a swarm of flies, so many that the sky turned black!

He sent a plague among the livestock of the land, but spared those belonging to the Hebrews. Then the Egyptians were afflicted with horrible boils. Next, God sent a terrible hailstorm which stripped the land, then those plants that had survived were consumed by a swarm of locusts. Nothing green remained on tree or plant in all the land of Egypt. After this, God sent total darkness to cover Egypt for three whole days.

Each time, Pharaoh pretended that he would relent, yet each time, once the plague was lifted, he refused to let the Hebrews go. The Lord hardened Pharaoh's heart to teach him a lesson, to show God's true power and to make sure the story was told throughout the world.

But now the time had come for the final plague. Moses warned Pharaoh that God would pass through the country at midnight and every first-born son in the land would die, from the son of Pharaoh himself, to the son of the lowliest slave girl, and even the first-born of the animals as well. But Pharaoh would not listen.

Moses told the Israelites what God wanted them to do to be spared. Each household was to kill a lamb and smear some of the blood on the door frame, and eat the meat in a special way.

That night, God passed throughout Egypt and the next day the land was filled with the sound of mourning, for all the first-born sons had died, even the son of mighty Pharaoh, but the Hebrews were spared.

Now the Egyptians couldn't get rid of the Hebrews quick enough, and so the Hebrews prepared to leave Egypt.

CROSSING THE RED SEA

The Hebrews travelled southwards across the desert, towards the Red Sea. By day, God sent a great column of cloud to guide them, and by night they followed a pillar of fire, but Pharaoh was regretting his decision to let them go, and had set off with his army to bring them back.

The Hebrews were terrified, for their way was barred by the waters of the Red Sea. But Moses did not give up his faith in God and stood firm. "God will look after us," he said confidently. "And he will crush our enemy."

Then God told Moses to raise his staff and stretch out his hand over the sea to divide the water so that the Israelites could go through the sea on dry ground.

Every one of the Israelites passed safely through the sea on dry ground, with a wall of water on their right and on their left!

But when the Egyptians followed them into the sea, God closed the waters together and the Egyptians were all swept under. Of all that mighty army, there were no survivors – not one horse, not one soldier!

And the people of Israel, safe on the other shore of the Red Sea, were filled with gratitude and relief. They sang and danced in their joy, and they knew that their God was both mighty and merciful, and they praised him greatly.

FOOD AND WATER IN THE DESERT

Moses led his people into the hot, dry desert. For three days they didn't find a drop of water, and when at last they did, it was too bitter to drink. They forgot what God had done for them, and began to complain angrily. God helped Moses to make the water drinkable, but they had to travel onwards, and soon they began to complain again. "Either we shall die of thirst or of starvation!" they wailed. "Why did you bring us out of Egypt to die?"

Once again, God helped his people. In the evenings, quail would come into the camp, and in the mornings, the ground would be covered with white flakes that tasted like wafers made with honey, which they called manna. For all the time that they were in the desert, God provided quail and manna for them, and God told Moses to take his staff and strike a rock, and from the rock flowed good, clear, fresh drinking water.

The people of Israel continued to wander through the desert for many years and the Lord provided them with both food and water.

THE TEN COMMANDMENTS

Moses led the people to Mount Sinai. There, God spoke to Moses and told him that if the people would honour and obey him, then he would always be with them. The elders agreed to do everything the Lord had told them. Then God told Moses that in three days he would appear to them on Mount Sinai.

On the morning of the third day, there was thunder and lightning, with a thick cloud over the mountain, and a loud trumpet blast. The people trembled and waited at the foot of the mountain. Then God called Moses to the top of it and spoke to him, saying: "I am the Lord your God, who brought you out of Egypt.

"You shall have no other gods before me.

"You shall not make any false idols.

"You shall not misuse my name.

"Remember the Sabbath and keep it holy.

"Honour your father and your mother.

"You shall not murder.

"You shall not commit adultery.

"You shall not steal.

"You shall not tell lies.

"You shall not envy anything that belongs to your neighbour."

Moses told the people what God had commanded and they promised to obey.

THE GOLDEN CALF

Moses was gone up the mountain for such a long time talking to God that the people began to believe he would never come back down. They asked Aaron to make them gods to lead them, and Aaron told them to gather all their gold jewellery and used it to make a beautiful golden calf, which he placed on an altar. The people gathered round and began to worship it.

God was angry with them and vowed to destroy them, but Moses pleaded with him to forgive them, and God relented. But when Moses went down from the mountain with the tablets, and saw the people singing and

dancing around the golden calf, he threw the tablets to the ground in fury, where they shattered. Next, he burned the calf and ground it to powder. God punished those who had sinned with a plague.

Now, God placed the commandments on two new stone tablets and the Israelites kept them in a special chest, known as the Ark of the Covenant. Wherever they went, they carried the Ark of the Covenant with them, and they felt the presence of the Lord.

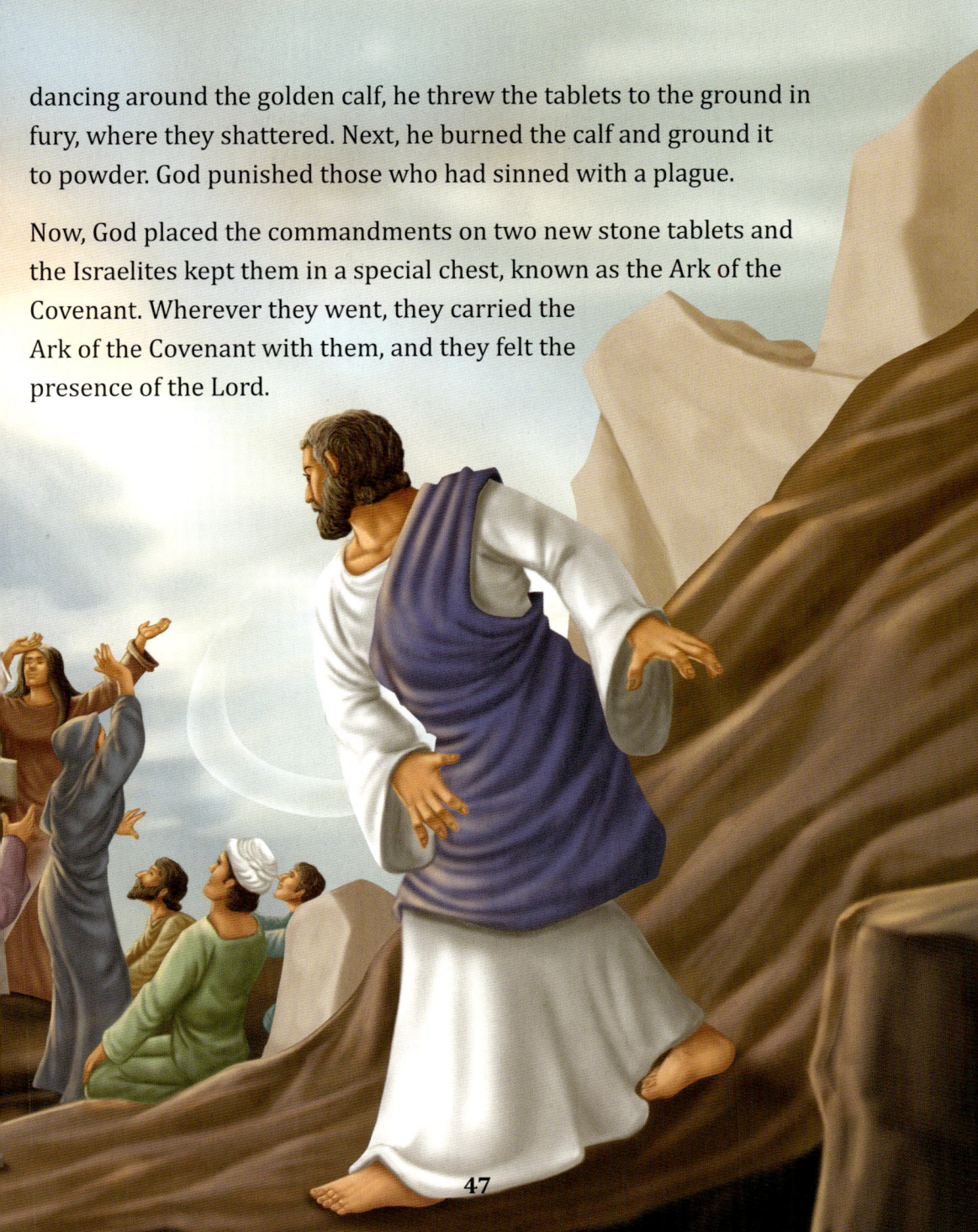

THE TWELVE SPIES

There came a time when God told Moses to send some men to explore Canaan, the land he intended for the Israelites. So Moses chose twelve men, one from each of the tribes that came from the sons of Jacob, and he sent them to find out what the land was like.

They came back laden with juicy fruit. "The land really does flow with milk and honey, just as God promised!" they enthused. But they also said that there were too many people living there, and that the cities were well defended. Only two of them, Caleb and Joshua, were brave enough and trusted God enough to believe they could take the land that God had promised them.

God was angry with the Israelites for not trusting him. He threatened to kill them all, but Moses pleaded on their behalf, and God relented. Still, he told them that not one of those who had doubted him would ever set foot in the Promised Land, and he struck down those men who had been sent to explore Canaan, and who had doubted him and spread their fear among the people of Israel. Finally, he cursed the rest of the doubting Israelites to wander the desert for another forty years!

WATER FROM A ROCK

However much God helped them, the Israelites never stopped grumbling and complaining, for they were still in the desert and were thirsty. Moses and Aaron asked God to help once more. God told them to take the staff and gather everyone before a large rock. "Speak to that rock before their eyes and it will pour out its water," he commanded them.

Moses and Aaron gathered the people. "Listen, you rebels, must we bring you water out of this rock?" Moses said, then struck the rock twice with his staff. Water gushed out, and everyone was able to drink.

But God was disappointed because Moses hadn't followed his instructions, nor had he given the credit to God, and so he told the brothers that they would never enter the Promised Land.

JOSHUA TAKES COMMAND

The years passed, and Moses was now very old. He called the people of Israel to him. "God has told me that I may not enter the Promised Land. Joshua will lead you there. You must be brave and strong, for God will not leave you," and he said to Joshua in front of all the people, "Be strong and courageous, for you must lead these people into the Promised Land and divide it among them. The Lord himself goes before you and will be with you; he will never leave you nor forsake you, so do not be afraid or discouraged."

God had some special words just for Joshua. "You will lead the people into the land I have promised them. Don't be afraid, Joshua, for I will always be with you."

It was time for Moses to leave his people. Before he went, he gathered them to him and said to them, "You are truly blessed! Who is like you, a people saved by the Lord? He is your shield and helper and your glorious sword. Your enemies will cower before you, and you will trample down their high places."

Moses climbed Mount Nebo, and the Lord showed him the whole land of Canaan in the distance. Moses died on the mountain and was gathered to his people. He was one hundred and twenty years old when he died, yet his eyes were not weak, nor was his strength gone. The people mourned for thirty days. They knew that there would never be another prophet like him, who had spoken with the Lord face to face.

THE WALLS OF JERICHO

For many years the Israelites had wandered in the harsh desert, but now it was time to cross the River Jordan into the Promised Land, where food and water were plentiful, and the land was green and lush.

The river was in flood, and there was no bridge or ford, but Joshua knew God would help them. He sent the priests ahead, carrying the Ark of the Covenant. As soon as their feet touched the water, it stopped flowing and made a huge wall, and a dry path stretched before them! The people of Israel began to cross safely over. By nightfall, they had safely arrived in the land promised to them by God for so long.

After thanking God, the Israelites laid siege to Jericho. The walls were tall and strong, but God told Joshua to have the armed men march around the city every day for six days, following the Ark and priests with trumpets. On the seventh day, the priests were to sound a long blast on the trumpets, and then all the people were to shout loudly. God told Joshua that the walls of the city would collapse, and Jericho would fall to them.

The Israelites did exactly as God commanded them, and on the seventh day, when the trumpets sounded, the people raised a mighty cry. Just as God had promised, the city walls trembled and then collapsed before them! The soldiers charged in and took the city. The story of how the Lord had helped Joshua take Jericho spread throughout the land!

THE SUN AND THE MOON

When the people of the nearby town of Gibeon heard how Jericho had fallen, they feared for their own lives. They decided to trick the Israelites into signing a peace treaty with them. Joshua and his men were taken in by the trickery, and didn't stop to ask for God's advice. Instead, Joshua drew up a peace treaty with the men of Gibeon on the spot, and swore an oath to keep it. They soon learned the truth, but they had sworn an oath in God's name and could not go back on their word.

Shortly afterwards, Gibeon came under attack. The Israelites went to their aid, for Joshua was an honourable man. God had not been pleased with him for signing the treaty, but he was pleased he was keeping his word.

Joshua and his army marched all through the night to get to Gibeon, and their enemies were caught by surprise. Throughout the battle, God was on their side. He sent great hailstones to fall on the enemy, and soon Joshua knew that the Israelites were winning – but he also knew that night would fall before they could finish the battle!

Then Joshua called out, "Sun, stand still over Gibeon, and you, moon, over the Valley of Aijalon!" and God listened to Joshua, and made the sun and the moon stand still until Joshua and his men had won the battle!

The people of Israel had many more battles to fight, but with God's help, the land was finally theirs.

GIDEON AND THE THREE HUNDRED

The terrible Midianites had taken over their land, and the Israelites cried out to God to help them. God sent a messenger to Gideon, to tell him he had been chosen to lead his people.

Gideon gathered many men to fight against the Midianites, but God told him he had too many. He told Gideon to send away any who were afraid – over two thirds of the men went home! But God told Gideon there were still too many of them. He told him to have the men drink from the river, and to take with him only those who cupped water in their hands. Now only three hundred men were left!

That night, Gideon looked down on the sea of Midianite tents – how could they ever beat them? There were so many of them! God knew he was anxious and told him to creep down to the enemy camp where he overheard the soldiers recounting bad dreams: "I dreamt that a round loaf of bread came tumbling into the camp, knocked into the tent and completely flattened it!" exclaimed one Midianite soldier to another.

"That will be the sword of Gideon!" wailed the second soldier. "God must have given the whole camp over into his hands!"

Gideon returned full of confidence. He roused his men, giving them all trumpets and empty jars with torches inside.

The men reached the edge of the camp and, following Gideon's signal, blew their trumpets, smashed the jars, and shouted out loud. The harsh noise and sudden light startled the Midianites so much that the camp fell into confusion, and the soldiers fled in terror, even turning on one another in their fright!

In this way, Gideon and God defeated the Midianites with just three hundred men!

SAMSON THE STRONG

For forty years the Israelites had been enslaved by their enemies. One day God sent a message to a man called Manoah and his wife: "You will have a son who will grow up to deliver you from the Philistines." When their son was born, they named him Samson, and they never once cut his hair. It was a sign that he belonged to God in a very special way.

One day when Samson was older, he was attacked by one of the fierce lions that roamed the land of Canaan. Samson was filled with the Spirit of the Lord, and he became so strong that he was able to kill the beast with his bare hands!

Samson was a thorn in the side of the Philistines. They hated and feared him, for he carried out many attacks against them. But when he fell in love with Delilah, a beautiful Philistine woman, they bribed her to discover the secret of Samson's strength.

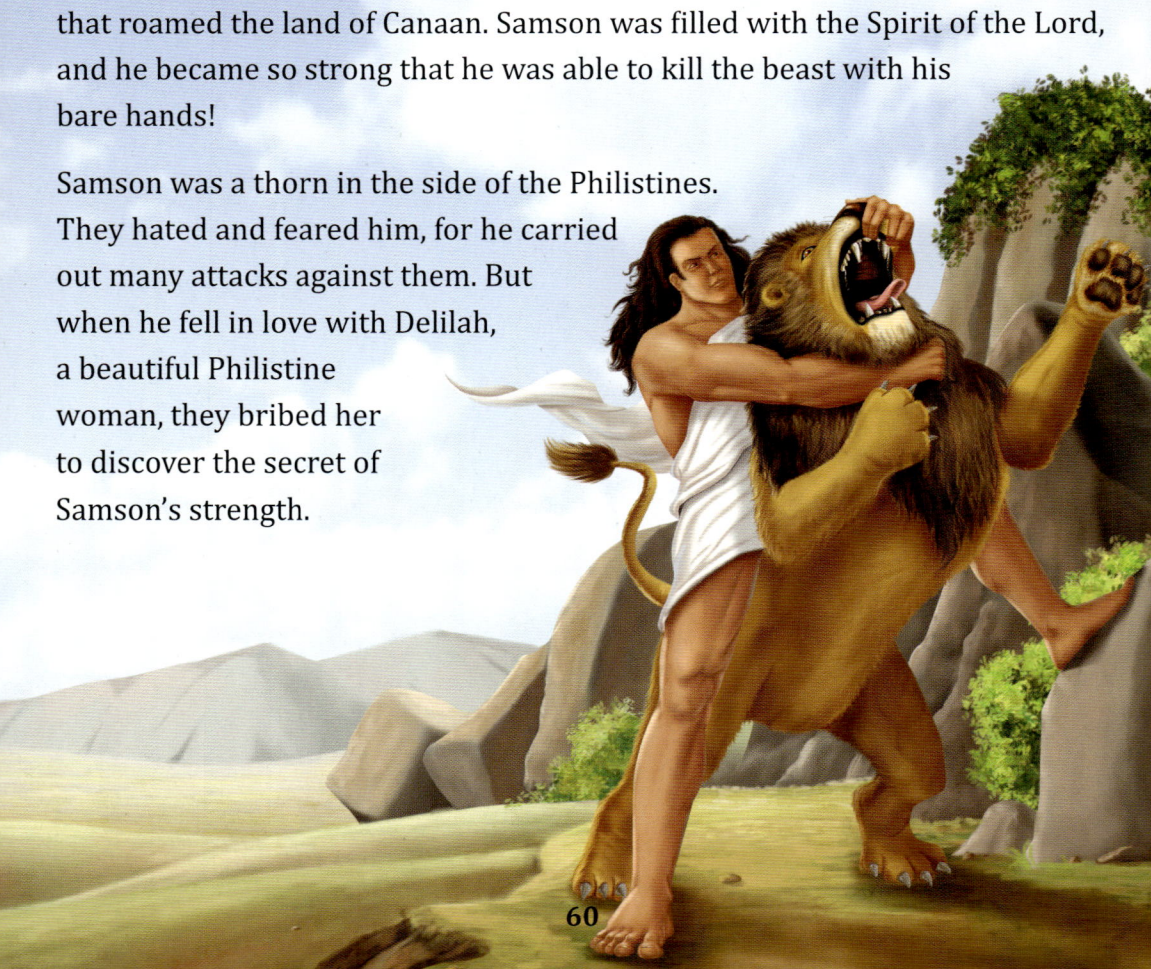

Treacherous Delilah found out that if anyone were to cut Samson's hair, he would lose all his strength, and so, one night, the Philistines crept into his room and cut off his hair as he slept. He was powerless when he awoke, and he could do nothing as they bound him and threw him into prison!

Over time, Samson's hair grew back. One day, the Philistine rulers were all gathered for a feast in a temple. Samson was brought to be made fun of. He was chained between the two central pillars of the temple.

Then Samson prayed to God with all his heart, "Give me strength just one more time, my Lord, so that I can take revenge upon my enemies!"

Once more, Samson was filled with strength. He pushed against the pillars with all his might and they toppled. The temple crashed down, killing everyone inside. Samson killed more of his enemies with this final act than he had killed in his entire life!

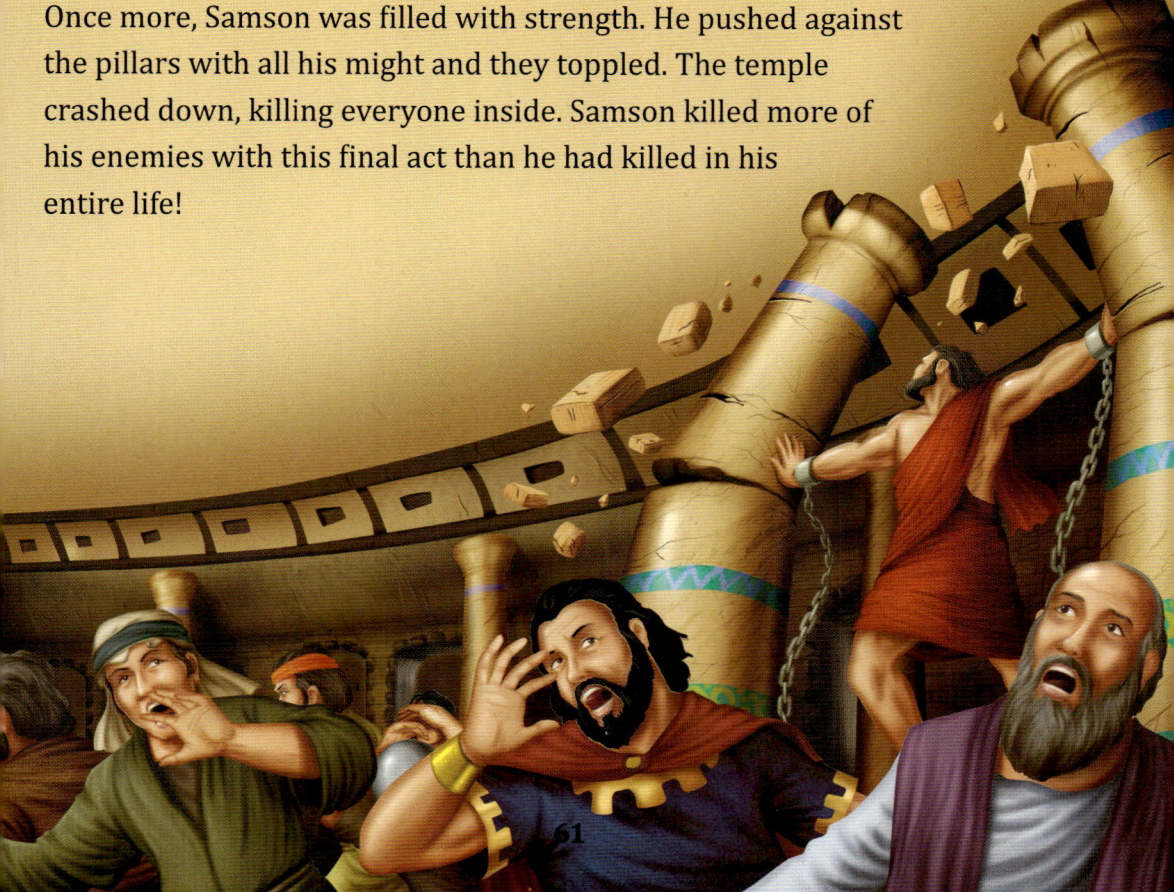

FAITHFUL RUTH

Many years ago, Naomi and her family had left their home in Bethlehem and moved to Moab. Her husband had died, but when her sons grew older, they married two lovely girls from Moab and brought them home to live. But now her sons had died too, and Naomi was alone in a foreign land.

Naomi wanted to go home to Bethlehem. She loved her two daughters-in-law, Orpah and Ruth, but she begged them to stay behind, for she was penniless and she knew her life would be hard.

Orpah and Ruth loved Naomi, and didn't want to part from her, but finally Orpah agreed to go home to her own mother.

Loyal Ruth, however, said, "Don't ask me to leave! I'll go wherever you go. Your people will be my people, and your God will be my God."

So it was that Ruth and Naomi came to Bethlehem. Soon they had no food left. Brave Ruth went out into the fields where workers were harvesting the crops and asked the owner, Boaz, if she could pick up any of the barley that his workers left behind. Boaz kindly let Ruth work in his fields and told his servants to share their food with her. When Ruth returned with a full basket of food, Naomi knew that the Lord was looking after them, for it turned out that Boaz was a relation of hers.

In time, Ruth married Boaz, and when they had a son, there was no happier woman in all of Bethlehem than Naomi!

HANNAH'S PRAYER

Hannah longed to have a child. She could think of nothing else. One day, when she was visiting the temple in Jerusalem, she went to the door of the holy tent and, weeping bitterly, began to pray. "Dear Lord, please give me a child, for I am so unhappy," she begged. "I swear that if you do, I will give him back to you to serve for all his life!" When Eli, the priest, saw Hannah and learnt of her troubles, he sent her on her way gently, saying, "May God answer your prayer."

Hannah left, feeling as if a great weight had left her shoulders. She had spoken to God – now he would decide what was best for her. And how thrilled she was when, some time later, she gave birth to a beautiful baby boy named Samuel!

She did not forget her promise to God, for when the boy was old enough, she took him to the temple, knowing he would be well looked after by the kind priest. Each year she visited him, and God, knowing how difficult it had been for her to give up her son, blessed her with more children to love and cherish at home.

As Samuel grew up, God often spoke to him, and in time people began to listen to what Samuel had to say.

THE SHEPHERD BOY

David was just a shepherd boy. He was the youngest of his family and he had many brothers who were older and stronger than he was. But God had chosen him as the future leader of Israel!

The Israelites were at war with the Philistines and the two armies had gathered to do battle. David had brought food to his brothers who were fighting in the army. The Philistines had a mighty champion. His name was Goliath and he was powerful and strong – and ten feet tall! Goliath had challenged the Israelite soldiers to single combat. Not one of them had dared to fight this terrible warrior. No one, that is, apart from David, for courage has nothing to do with size, and David knew that he had someone very special on his side – the Lord!

The king offered David his own armour and weapons, but they were too big and heavy for the young boy, so David stood before Goliath, with nothing but his staff, a sling, and five smooth stones from a nearby stream.

Goliath laughed when he saw the young shepherd boy, but David fearlessly ran towards him, putting a stone in his sling and flinging it with all his might. It hit Goliath in the middle of his forehead and when he fell to the ground, David raced up and, drawing out Goliath's own sword, cut his head from his body with one strike! The Philistines were so shocked when they saw their champion killed that they turned and ran away!

As for David, he went on to become a great king, despite starting life as a shepherd boy!

THE WISDOM OF SOLOMON

When King David died, his son Solomon was crowned king. Soon after, God spoke to Solomon in a dream and told him he would give him whatever he asked for. Solomon answered humbly, "I would like to be a great king like my father, but I am young and don't know how. Please give me wisdom to rule over your people wisely and do as you would have me do."

God was pleased with Solomon's answer. He told him, "I will give you wisdom. But I will also give you those things you did not ask for. You will be rich and respected, and if you follow in my ways, you will live a long life."

Solomon awoke comforted and strengthened, knowing God was by his side.

One day, two women came before Solomon holding a baby. They both claimed that the baby was theirs – that the other woman's child had died, and she had replaced the dead child with the living one.

Solomon looked at the women, and then told his guard to cut the child in two and give half to one woman and half to the other. The woman whose child it really was cried out in horror, "No! No, my lord! Give her the baby! Don't kill him! I would rather she looked after him than he died!" But the other woman said they should do as the king said, for that was fair.

Then the king gave his ruling: "Give the baby to the first woman. Do not kill him; she is his true mother." When all Israel heard the verdict the king had given, they saw how wise and clever God had made him.

GOD'S TEMPLE

King Solomon soon began to build the temple that his father David had once dreamed of building. He sent for the finest cedar wood, and the stones were cut at the quarry, so that hammers and chisels would not be heard on the holy site. The temple was wide and long and tall, with many chambers, and the most sacred of all was the Inner Temple.

The temple took thousands of men seven years to build, and when it was finished, Solomon filled it with fine treasures. But the finest treasure of all was the chest of the Covenant, containing the two stone tablets. It was placed in the Inner Temple, where it rested under the wings of two golden cherubim, each fifteen feet high, their wings touching in the middle of the room.

The cloud of God's presence filled the temple and the people were full of wonder and gratitude. Then Solomon thanked God. "I know that you who created heaven and earth would never live in a building made by man, but I pray that here we can be close to you and hear your word."

God told him that he had heard his prayer, that his heart and eyes would be in the temple, and that as long as the king walked in God's ways and kept his laws, he would be with him.

ELIJAH AND THE RAVENS

Many years passed. Wicked King Ahab and his cruel wife Jezebel ruled over the northern kingdom of Israel, for the country was now divided. They built a temple for Baal, and killed many prophets. But God's prophet Elijah was not scared. He warned the king, "For the next few years there will be neither rain nor even dew in this land. You will learn that my God is the one true God," and it happened as he said.

It was no longer safe for Elijah to stay in Israel. God sent him east of the River Jordan. There, every morning and every evening ravens brought him bread and meat, and he drank from a small brook.

But the drought continued, and at last even the brook dried up completely. Then God told Elijah it was time for him to go to Sidon where a widow would help him.

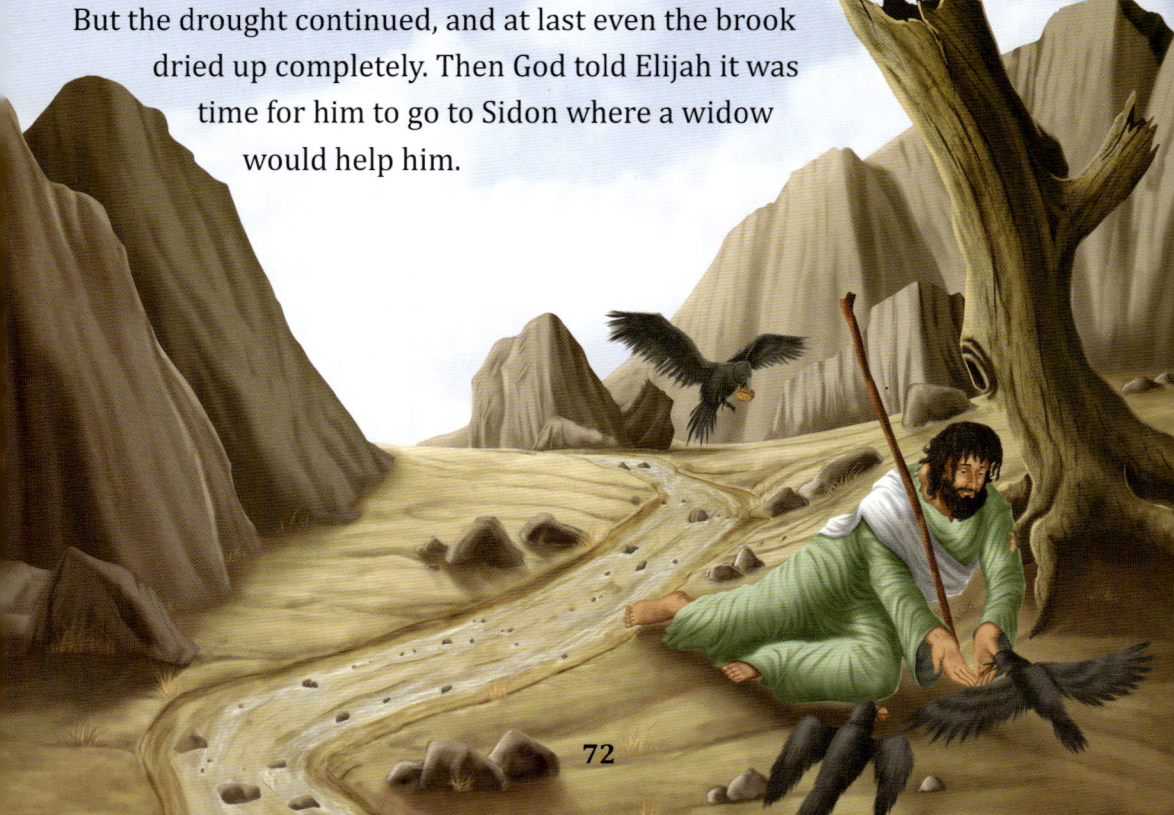

When Elijah reached the city gates of Sidon, he met a woman gathering firewood. He asked her for a drink of water. The kind widow went to fetch him a jar of water, even though water was scarce. As she was going, Elijah asked her for some bread.

"I'm afraid I have no bread," she sighed, "I have only a handful of flour in a jar and a little olive oil in a jug. I'm gathering a few sticks to take home and make one last meal for myself and my son."

Elijah told her not to worry, but to go home and make a small loaf of bread for him, and then one for herself and her son, for God had promised that the flour and oil would not run out until the day that rain fell on the land.

The kind widow did as Elijah had asked, and found that when she had made one loaf, she still had enough flour and oil to make another, and so it went on, day after day, and there was always enough food for Elijah, and for the widow and her son.

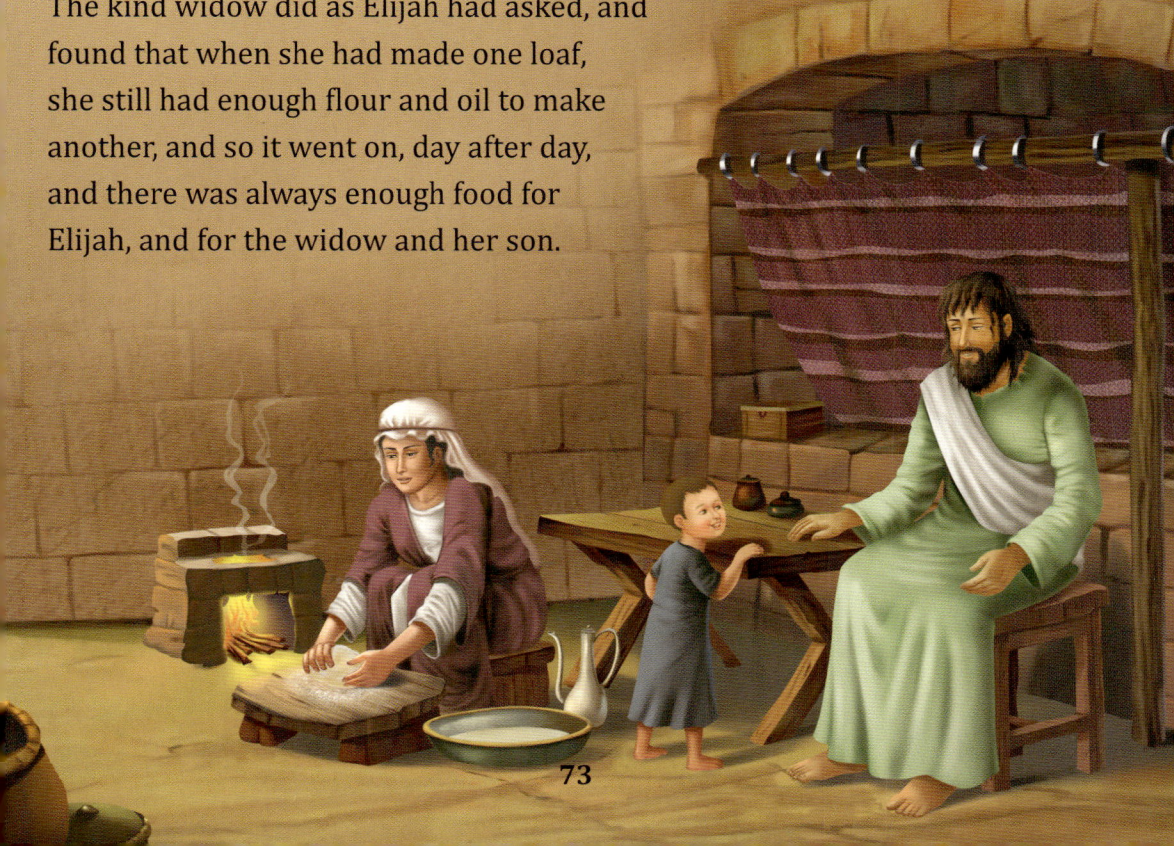

THE GREAT CONTEST

Three years passed without rain, and King Ahab was desperate. Elijah told him to gather the people of Israel and the prophets of Baal at Mount Carmel. "It is time for you to learn who is the true God of Israel!" he said, and he proposed a test. Both he and the prophets of Baal would prepare a bull for sacrifice. Then each would call upon their god to answer with fire! There were four hundred and fifty prophets of Baal – and Elijah!

Everyone watched eagerly as the many priests of Baal prepared their bull and then called upon their god to send fire. They prayed and prayed, but nothing happened. They danced frantically around the altar calling Baal's name, but nothing happened. They tore their clothes and slashed themselves with swords and spears, but still nothing happened.

"Perhaps Baal hasn't heard you," mocked Elijah. "Try harder!"

But try as they might, there was no answer or sign, and at last they fell to the ground in exhaustion.

Now Elijah went to the broken altar of the Lord, and used twelve stones, one for each of the tribes, to build an altar around which he dug a deep trench. He prepared the bull and laid it on the wood, then he told the people to fill four large jars with water and pour it on the sacrifice and the wood. When they had done this, he told them to do it again, and then again, until the altar was drenched and water filled the trench.

Then Elijah stepped forward and prayed: "Lord, the God of Abraham, Isaac, and Israel, let it be known today that you are God in Israel and that I have done these things at your command."

Then the fire of the Lord fell and burned up the sacrifice, the wood, the stones, and even the water!

The people fell to their knees. "It's true!" they cried. "The Lord is God!"

TAKEN TO HEAVEN

Elijah and his disciple Elisha were walking by the River Jordan. Elijah was old, and it was time to hand over his work to Elisha. He took off his cloak and struck the water with it. A path opened up before them, and they walked across. Then Elijah turned to his companion, saying, "Soon, I shall leave you. Is there anything you would ask of me before I go?"

Elisha thought carefully. "I should like to inherit your spirit, your greatness and power, to help me carry on your work," he replied humbly.

Suddenly a chariot of fire drawn by horses of fire appeared before them. Elisha looked on amazed as Elijah was taken up to heaven in a whirlwind!

When the sky was empty once again, Elisha noticed that Elijah's cloak had fallen to the ground. He picked it up and walked to the riverbank. He struck the river with the cloak, and the waters parted before him! When the other prophets saw what happened, they bowed low. "The spirit of Elijah has been passed on to Elisha!" they said in wonder.

WASHED CLEAN

Naaman, the general of the armies of Syria, was struck with a dreadful skin disease. An Israelite slave girl told him that the wonderful prophet, Elisha, in Samaria might be able to help, so Naaman travelled to Israel.

When Naaman reached Elisha's house, he expected the prophet to come out and perform a miracle. Instead, Elisha sent his servant out to tell the general to bathe in the River Jordan seven times, and he would be cured.

Naaman was offended. "Why should I wash in that filthy river?" he shouted. "We have plenty of rivers in Syria!" He would have left in disgust had his servant not calmed him down!

Realising he was being foolish, Naaman went to the river and bathed in it – when he emerged after the seventh time, his skin was soft and smooth!

He went to thank Elisha. "Yours is the true God. From now on I'll worship him," and he offered Elisha a gift. Elisha would take nothing, but his servant went after the general secretly, saying Elisha had changed his mind. Naaman gave him money which the servant hid under his bed. But Elisha knew what had happened. "For your greed and lies you will be punished," he said sternly. "You will suffer from the same disease Naaman had!"

JEHOSHAPHAT TRUSTS GOD

King Jehoshaphat had gathered all the people of Judah to Jerusalem. A vast army was on its way to destroy the land. But Jehoshaphat didn't despair – he knew who to talk to! He called his people together to pray to God for help.

As they prayed together, the Spirit of the Lord came on one of the priests and he said, "God says: 'Don't be afraid, for this is God's battle, not yours. Go out to face your enemy tomorrow, and the Lord will be with you.'"

So the next morning, the army of Judah set out for the battlefield, singing God's praises as they went. But as they marched, God made the different groups of the enemy army fight against themselves, and by the time the soldiers of Judah came to the place where they had expected to give battle, all they saw before them was a sea of dead bodies! No one had escaped!

The neighbouring kingdoms were filled with fear at this sign of God's power and for a while, the people of Judah lived in peace.

HEZEKIAH'S PRAYER

The years passed and Israel fell into disgrace. The city of Samaria, capital of the northern kingdom, fell to Assyria, and the Israelites were forced to leave their country and march to a far off land.

Further south, Hezekiah was king of Judah. He was a good man and trusted in God alone for protection. Before long, the mighty army of Assyria came before the walls of Jerusalem and demanded that the city surrender. The people cowered in fear, but the prophet Isaiah said, "Do not be afraid. Do not make the same mistake as Israel. Trust in God, for he will save us."

The enemy commander sent another message. "Your God will not save you. He did not save Samaria! Give up now, and I will be merciful!"

Hezekiah prayed to God. "You are the only true God," he said. "I place all my trust in you. Deliver us now so that all the kingdoms may know that you alone, Lord, are God."

That night the angel of the Lord passed through the Assyrian camp, and when the sun came up the next morning, it rose on the dead bodies of thousands and thousands of Assyrian soldiers. Those Assyrians still alive left as quickly as they could!

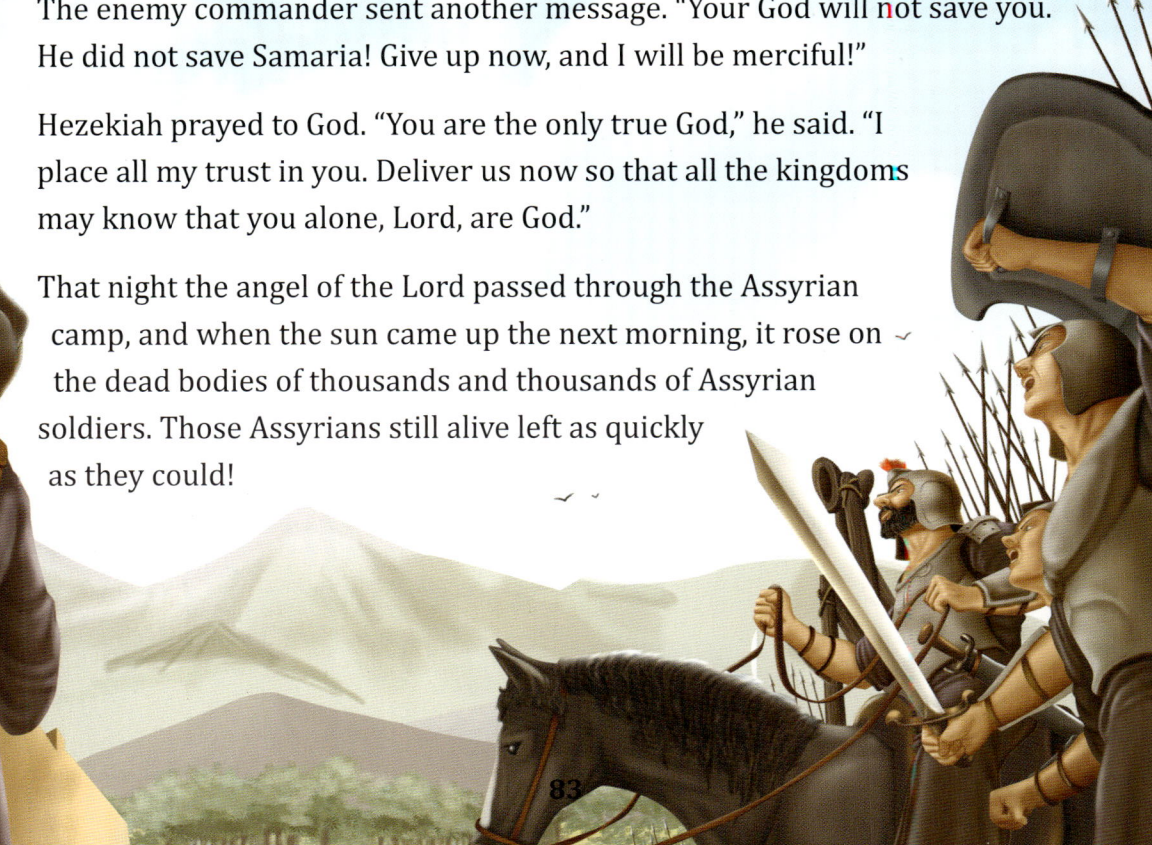

THE POTTER'S CLAY

One of the greatest prophets of the Lord was Jeremiah. He was chosen by God to pass on his message to the kings and people of Judah in a very difficult time. When Jeremiah first heard God speak to him, he thought he was far too young to be a prophet. But God said, "Don't worry. I will be with you, and I will put the words into your mouth."

Jeremiah watched a potter mould pieces of rough clay into beautiful vases and useful jugs. Sometimes the clay didn't do what the potter wanted it to, so he would start again and make it into something different. "Israel is like the clay," God said. "If Israel does evil, I will change whatever good thing I had planned for it, but if Israel repents, then I will relent."

God told Jeremiah to warn the people that disaster was coming, and that only by being truly sorry could they stop it. Jeremiah took some priests and elders to the Valley of Ben Hinnom. He warned them that God was going to punish his people for their wrongdoing. Jeremiah broke a clay jar into many pieces and said, "God will smash this nation and this city just like this jar."

The priests were so cross that they threw Jeremiah into prison!

THE FALL OF JERUSALEM

The ruler of Jerusalem refused to listen to Jeremiah's warnings, and tried to rebel against Nebuchadnezzar of Babylon. It was time for God to punish his disobedient children. The Babylonians attacked and destroyed the city. They set fire to the temple, the palace and all the houses, and the rest of the people were taken away as slaves.

But God hadn't stopped loving his children. Years before, Isaiah the prophet had known this would happen, and had a message of hope for the exiles from God: "'Comfort my people,' says your God. 'Speak tenderly to Jerusalem, and tell her she has paid for her sins.' God tends his flock like a shepherd. He gathers the lambs and carries them close to his heart. So never believe he doesn't care about you!"

Jeremiah, too, wrote a letter to the exiles to comfort them and give them hope: "This is what the Lord says: 'When seventy years are completed, I will bring you back to this place. You will pray to me, and I will listen. You will seek me and find me when you seek with all your heart, and I will bring you back from captivity. I will gather you from all the places where I have banished you, and will bring you back to the place from which I carried you into exile.'"

God knew that his children would learn from their lesson. They would once again learn to love and worship him and follow his ways, and then they would return home, with God by their side. But for now, they were slaves in a foreign country.

THE FIERY FURNACE

Daniel and his friends were exiles in Babylon, but because they came from good families they had been well-treated and educated, and had become advisors to the king himself, for God was with them.

One day, King Nebuchadnezzar decided to have a great statue built out of gold, ninety feet high and nine feet wide. When it was completed, a special ceremony was held, and a herald demanded that everyone bow down and worship the statue, under pain of death!

Among the crowd were Daniel's three friends, Shadrach, Meshach and Abednego, who refused to bow down before the statue, for to do so would be to disobey God's commandment to worship him alone.

When the king learnt of the three men's defiance, he was furious. He offered them one more chance to obey, but the young men still refused, saying, "Your Majesty, we won't bow down to anyone but our God. He can save us from the furnace, but even if he doesn't, we will never worship your statue."

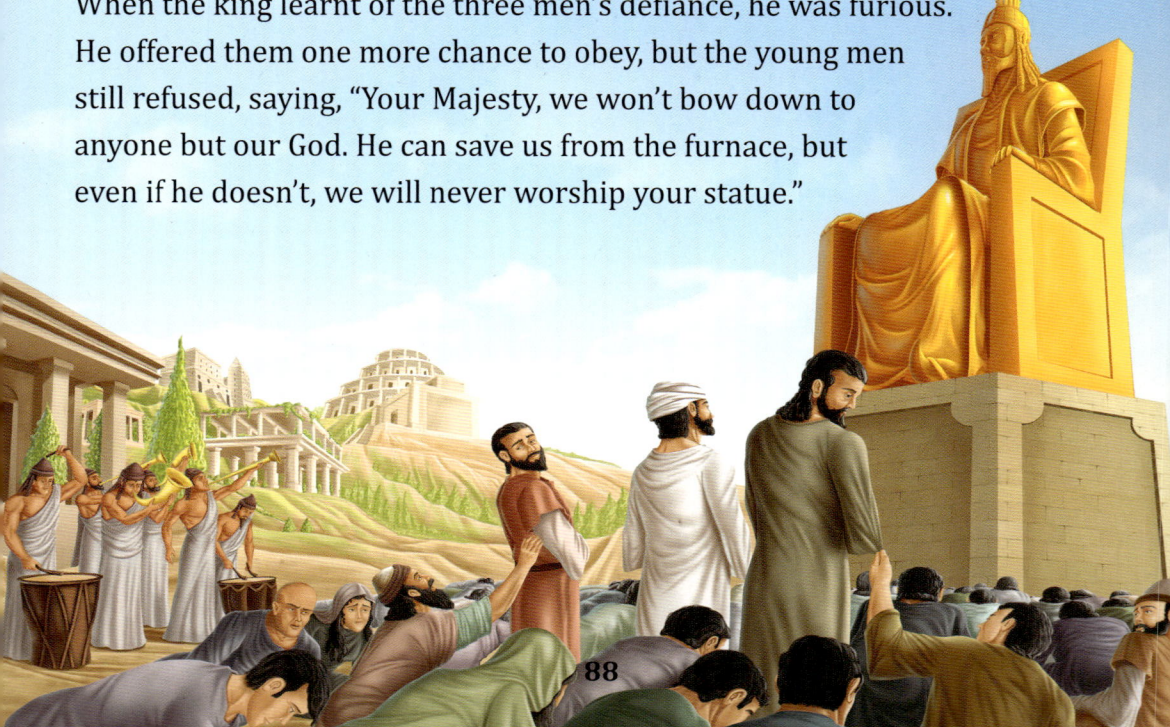

The angry king told his guards to tie them up with ropes, and to stoke up the furnace until it was seven times hotter than usual. Then they were thrown into the flames. The furnace was so hot that the guards themselves were scorched to death!

Nebuchadnezzar looked on. Suddenly he leapt up in disbelief, for within the furnace he could see four men: Shadrach, Meshach and Abednego were no longer bound, but walked around freely, and with them was a fourth man who looked like the Son of God!

The king called to the men to come out of the fire, and the friends walked out unharmed. Their skin was not burned, their clothes were not singed. Nebuchadnezzar was amazed. "Your God is indeed great, for he sent an angel to rescue his servants who were willing to give up their lives to follow his commands. He should be praised. No other god could do this!"

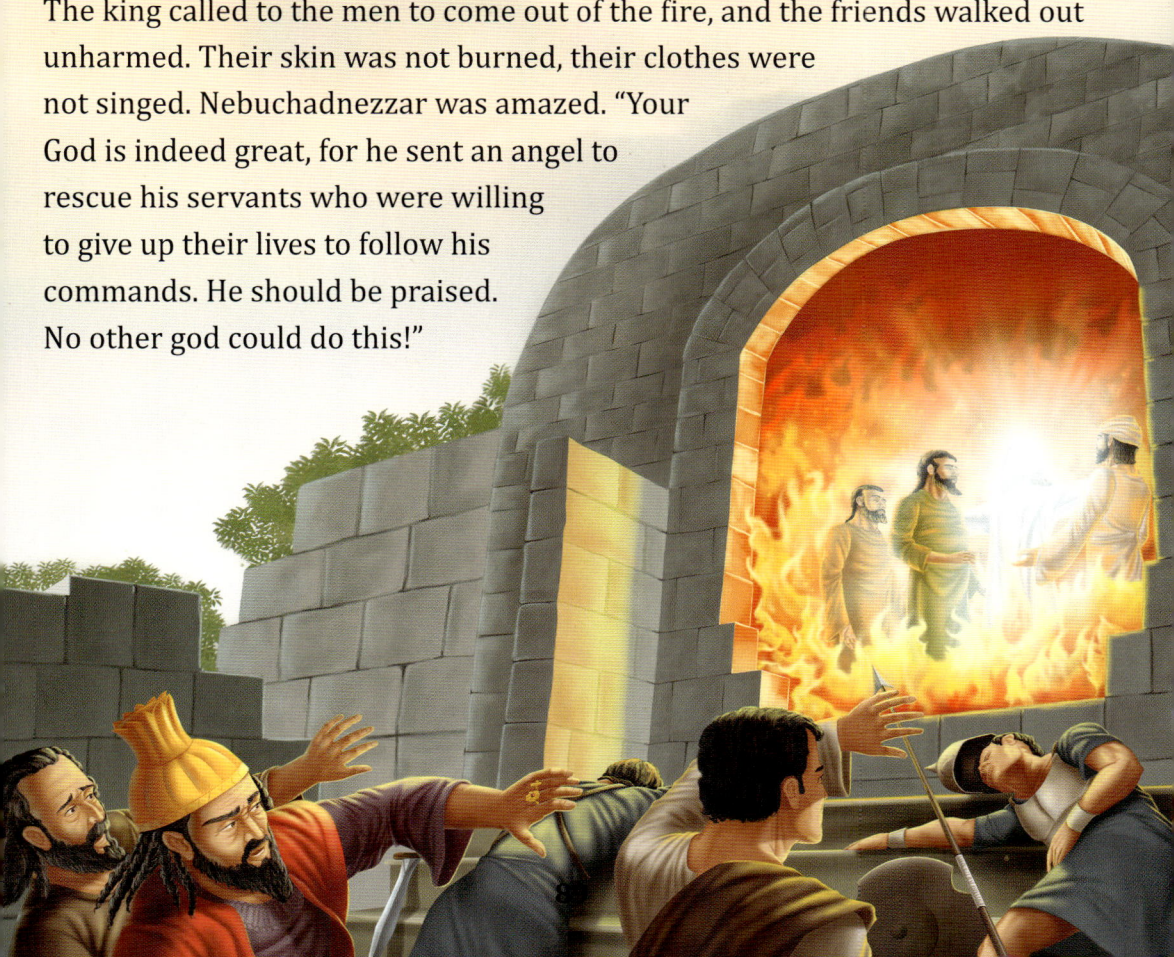

DANIEL IN THE LIONS' DEN

The new king, Darius was impressed with Daniel, for he was wise and honest, and soon Darius put him in charge of the kingdom. The other officials were jealous and set a trap. They knew Daniel prayed to his God every day at his window, and they advised the king to approve a new law stating that no one should pray to anyone other than the king.

Daniel prayed just as he had always done. He would not stop praying to God, or even hide what he was doing. The king's advisors demanded that Daniel be thrown to the lions, according to the law. "I hope your God can save you," said the king sadly, as Daniel was thrown to the lions.

At first light, Darius rushed down to the pit. "Daniel!" he cried out, more in desperation than hope. "Has your God been able to save you?"

He could not believe his ears when Daniel answered, "My God sent an angel and shut the mouths of the lions. They have not hurt me, for I was found innocent. Nor have I ever wronged you." The king was overjoyed and had Daniel brought out immediately. Then he ordered the men who had tricked him to be thrown into the pit themselves – and this time the lions were ruthless!

After this, Darius ordered his people to respect and honour Daniel's God: "For he can do wonderful things in heaven and on earth, and he rescued Daniel from the power of the lions!"

RETURN TO JERUSALEM

When Daniel was an old man, King Cyrus took the throne. His Persian empire stretched far and wide, but God touched his heart and the mighty king issued a decree that the exiles from Judah could at last return home. He also sent for the precious treasures taken from God's temple so many years ago, and gave them to the exiles to take back.

Great was the excitement and the rejoicing among the people. They couldn't believe they were finally going to return home! But not everybody was able to return to Jerusalem. The journey would be long and hard, and it would take time to rebuild the temple and city. Only the strongest and fittest were able to go.

Daniel was one of those who stayed behind. But his heart was filled with joy as he saw his people set out on their way, singing praises to God and laughing and smiling, and he gave thanks to God for allowing his people to return home and start again.

REBUILDING THE WALLS

Nehemiah was in Babylon. The temple had been rebuilt in Jerusalem, but the walls were still ruined, and people were still struggling. The emperor gave him permission to go back to his homeland and help rebuild the city, but things were even worse than he had expected – the walls were reduced to rubble and the people in neighbouring Samaria were doing everything they could to discourage the Jews. Still, Nehemiah gathered the people together and told them that God would be with them.

Work started, and everyone who could helped out on the walls. The Samaritans were worried. They didn't want Jerusalem to be strong and safe, so they plotted an attack. But Nehemiah divided his men into two –

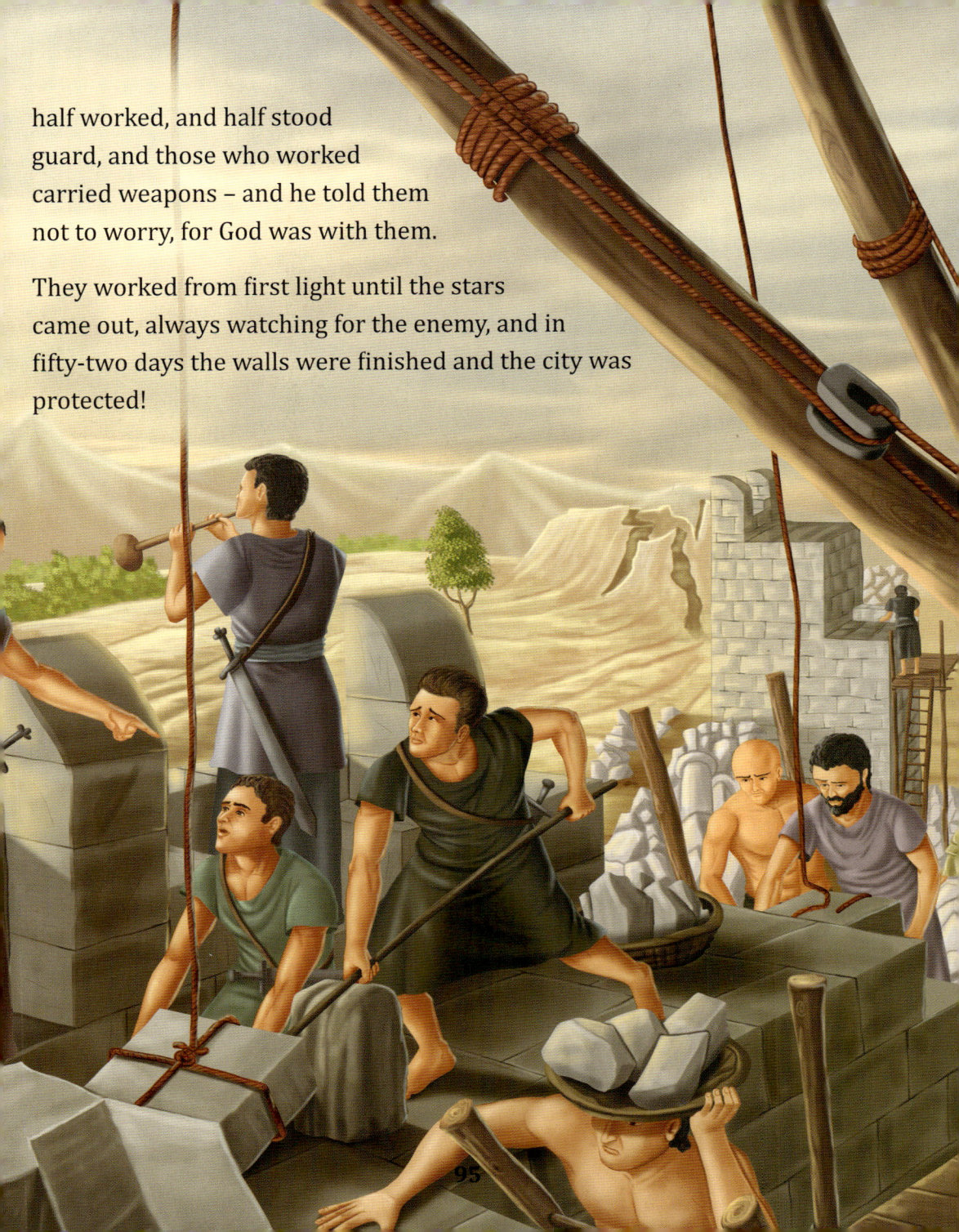

half worked, and half stood guard, and those who worked carried weapons – and he told them not to worry, for God was with them.

They worked from first light until the stars came out, always watching for the enemy, and in fifty-two days the walls were finished and the city was protected!

BEAUTIFUL ESTHER

King Xerxes was in search of a new queen, and so servants were sent out to find all the beautiful young maidens of the land and bring them to the palace. Amongst them was a lovely young girl named Esther, and as soon as King Xerxes saw her, he declared that she would be his wife. Esther didn't tell him she was a Jew.

Esther's cousin, Mordecai, refused to bow to the prime minister, a cruel, proud man named Haman. Haman was angry, and when he found out that Mordecai was a Jew, he decided to punish not only him, but all the other Jews as well, tricking the king into signing a law that said that any people in the kingdom who did not obey the king should be put to death.

The king agreed, and so Haman sent out a royal decree, stating that on the thirteenth day of the twelfth month of that year, all Jews – young and old, women and children – were to be killed throughout the empire!

THE BRAVE QUEEN

Mordecai begged that Esther plead their case before the king. She was terrified, for she could be killed for going to the king without a summons! But although she was scared, she went before King Xerxes, and to her relief, he smiled when he saw her and said, "Tell me what you want and you shall have it – even if it is half my empire!"

Esther could not bring herself to ask the king there and then, but invited him and Haman to a banquet in her rooms.

During the banquet, the king again asked Esther what it was that she wanted. This time, the queen was brave enough to ask, "Your Majesty, if I have found favour in your sight, I beg you to save my life and that of my people, for we have been sold for slaughter!"

"Who has dared to do such a thing?" roared the king, and Esther pointed to Haman, who threw himself at her feet and begged for his life. The king was furious and ordered that Haman be killed!

Then, although he could not overturn the law, the king sent out another decree saying that all Jews might arm themselves, and if attacked, they might fight back and destroy the attackers and take all their possessions. So when the followers of Haman tried to massacre the Jewish people, the Jews fought back and destroyed them utterly. Thanks to brave Esther and her cousin Mordecai, the Jewish people were saved!

JONAH AND THE BIG FISH

Jonah was a prophet. One day, God told him to go to Nineveh, and tell the people that, unless they turned from their wicked ways, God would destroy their city. Now, the people of Nineveh were enemies of the Jews, and Jonah didn't want to warn them. He thought they deserved to be punished! In fact, he boarded a ship heading in the opposite direction! He was trying to run away from God, but of course, God is everywhere!

A dreadful storm sprang up from nowhere. The winds howled and the waves towered above the ship. The terrified sailors threw their cargo over the side to lighten the ship, and they prayed to their gods.

The sailors drew straws to see who had angered the gods. Jonah picked the short straw! He confessed that he was running away from God, and that he was being punished. He realised how foolish he had been, and told them to cast him overboard, for God was only angry with him. With heavy hearts, the sailors lowered Jonah over the side. Instantly, the sea was calm! They were filled with awe, and began to pray to God with all their hearts.

Jonah sank swiftly to the bottom of the sea, but before he could take his last breath, God sent an enormous fish which swallowed Jonah whole, and there inside the fish Jonah was safe. For three days and nights, Jonah sat inside the fish. He had plenty of time to think about his mistakes and to feel sorry for having disobeyed God. He prayed to God, thanking him for his mercy and letting him know how remorseful he felt.

After three days, God commanded the fish to spit Jonah up, unharmed, onto dry land. And when God asked him again to take his message to Nineveh, Jonah was ready to do his will.

THE NEW TESTAMENT

A VISIT FROM AN ANGEL

Many centuries had passed since the Jews had rebuilt Jerusalem. Now King Herod sat on the throne of Judah, but he answered to Augustus Caesar, the emperor of the mighty Roman empire. In Nazareth in Galilee there lived a good and gentle girl who loved God. Her name was Mary. She was engaged to a carpenter called Joseph.

One day, an angel appeared to Mary. "Don't be afraid," he told the startled girl. "God has chosen you for a very special honour. You will give birth to a son, and you are to call him Jesus. He will be called the Son of God, and his kingdom will never end!"

Mary was filled with wonder. "How can this be?" she asked softly. "I'm not even married!"

"Everything is possible for God," replied the angel gently. "The Holy Spirit will come on you, and your child will be God's own son."

Mary bowed her head humbly, and said, "It will be as God wills it."

BORN IN A MANGER

Around this time, the emperor of Rome ordered a census of all the people he ruled over. All the people throughout the lands ruled by Rome had to go to their hometown to be counted. Mary and Joseph had to travel to Bethlehem, the town of Joseph's ancestor, King David. It was a long journey and took several days.

By the time they arrived, they were tired and desperately wanted to find a room for the night, for it was clear that the time had come for Mary's baby to be born. But the town was filled to bursting with people who had come to Bethlehem because of the census. Every inn was full!

Even though poor Mary badly needed to find somewhere to stay, there was no room for them anywhere. In the end, an innkeeper showed them to a room where the animals were kept, and it was in this humble place that Mary's baby was born.

She wrapped him in strips of cloth, then laid him gently on clean straw in a manger – the feeding trough from which the animals would have eaten.

Mary and Joseph looked down upon their son with joy, and they named him Jesus, just as the angel had told them to.

THE SHEPHERDS' STORY

That same night, some shepherds were watching over their sheep in the hills above Bethlehem. Suddenly, an angel of the Lord appeared to them and the dark sky was ablaze with light!

As the shepherds fell to the ground in fear, the angel said, "Don't be afraid. I have brought you good news. Today, in the town of David, a Saviour has been born to you; he is the Messiah, the Lord. Go and see for yourselves. You will find him wrapped in cloths, lying in a manger."

Then the sky was filled with angels praising God:

> *"Glory to God in the highest heaven,*
> *and peace on earth and good will to all men."*

When the angels had left, the shepherds looked at one another in amazement. They could hardly believe what had just happened! It didn't take long at all for them to make up their minds to go and see the baby with their very own eyes. So the shepherds hurried down to Bethlehem where they found the baby lying in a manger just as they had been told.

They knelt before him in wonder, and told Joseph and Mary what the angels had said to them. When they left, Mary spent much time thinking about what had happened, while the shepherds themselves rushed off to tell everyone about this special baby and the wonderful news!

THE BRIGHT STAR

In a distant land, three wise men had been studying the stars. When a really bright star was discovered shining in the skies, they followed it all the way to Judah, for they believed it was a sign that a great king had been born.

They went first to the court of King Herod, and asked if he could show them the way to the baby who would be the king of the Jews. Worried Herod called for his advisors, and they told him that a prophet had foretold that the new king would be born in the city of King David, in Bethlehem.

The cunning king directed the wise men to Bethlehem, saying, "Once you have found him, come back and tell me where he is, so that I can visit him, too."

The wise men followed the star to Bethlehem, where they found baby Jesus in a humble house. They knelt before him, and presented him with fine gifts of gold, frankincense and myrrh before returning home. But they did not stop off at Herod's palace, for God had warned them in a dream not to go there.

"MY FATHER'S HOUSE"

Herod was furious when he realised the wise men weren't coming back. He planned to kill this threat to his own power, but an angel warned Joseph in a dream and so the family fled to Egypt until Herod died and it was safe to return. Then they came back to Nazareth, and as the years passed, Jesus grew to be filled with grace and wisdom.

When Jesus was about twelve years old, his mother and father took him to Jerusalem to celebrate Passover – the festival which reminded the Jews of how God had rescued them from slavery in Egypt so many years before. For one whole week the city was filled to bursting.

At the end of this time, Mary and Joseph set off home with a host of other people, but on the way, they realised Jesus was missing. Frantic with worry, they rushed back to the crowded city to search for him. At last, on the third day of searching, they found him in the temple courts, talking with the teachers of the law, who were amazed by how much he knew.

"Jesus!" cried his parents. "We've been so worried about you!"

"But why?" answered the young boy. "Surely you knew that I would be in my Father's house?" Jesus loved Mary and Joseph dearly, but he understood that God was his Father in a very special way.

JESUS IS BAPTISED

Jesus' cousin, John, was living in the desert when God called him to prepare the world for the coming of his Son. John travelled throughout the land preaching. He told people that they needed to truly repent, and to change their ways, and they came from all around to listen. Many were truly sorry, and John baptised them in the River Jordan, as a sign that their sins had been washed away and that they could start afresh.

At that time, Jesus came from Nazareth to the River Jordan where John was preaching. John knew at once that this was the promised King, the Lamb of God. So when Jesus asked him to baptise him, John was shocked.

"You shouldn't be asking me to baptise you!" he protested. "I should be asking you to baptise me!" But Jesus insisted.

Just as Jesus was coming up from the water, the heavens opened, the Spirit descended on him like a dove, and a voice came from heaven, "You are my Son, whom I love; with you I am well pleased."

TESTED IN THE DESERT

Jesus spent forty days and nights in the dry, hot desert as a test. He ate nothing and was desperately hungry. The devil came to him and said, "If you are the Son of God, surely you can do anything. Why don't you tell these stones to become bread?"

Jesus answered calmly, "It is written: 'Man shall not live on bread alone, but on every word that comes from the mouth of God.'" Jesus knew that food wasn't the most important thing in life.

The devil took Jesus to the top of a temple and told him to throw himself off, for surely angels would rescue him. But Jesus said, "It is also written: 'Do not put the Lord your God to the test.'"

From a high mountain the devil offered him all the kingdoms of the world, if Jesus would simply bow down and worship him, but Jesus replied, "Away from me, Satan! For it is written: 'Worship the Lord your God, and serve him alone.'"

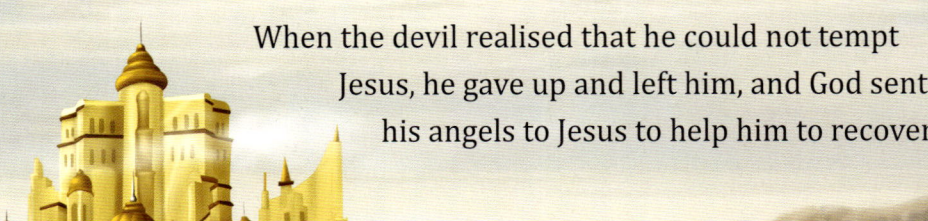

When the devil realised that he could not tempt Jesus, he gave up and left him, and God sent his angels to Jesus to help him to recover.

FISHING FOR MEN

Now Jesus returned to Galilee and began to preach. Word soon spread, and people travelled to hear him. One day, on the shore of Lake Galilee, the crowd was so large that Jesus asked a fisherman if he would take him out in his boat a little way, so everyone could see him.

Afterwards, Jesus told Simon, the fisherman, to take the boat out further and let down his nets. "Master," Simon answered, "we were out all night and caught nothing. But if you say so, then we will try again."

He couldn't believe his eyes when he pulled up his nets full of fish! He called to his brother Andrew, and to his friends James and John to help, and soon the two boats were so full of fish that they were ready to sink!

Simon fell to his knees, but Jesus smiled. "Don't be afraid, Simon. From now on you shall be called Peter for that is what you will be." (The name Peter comes from the Greek word for rock).

Then he turned to all the fishermen. "I want you to leave your nets," he said, "and come with me and fish for men instead, so that we can spread the good news!" The men pulled the boats up on the beach, left everything, and followed Jesus!

In time, Jesus chose eight more men to be his special followers or disciples. He chose them to carry on his work after his time on this world was over – to heal people, and to teach them about God's kingdom. In time, they would become known as his apostles, or messengers, for Jesus chose them to pass on his message of good news

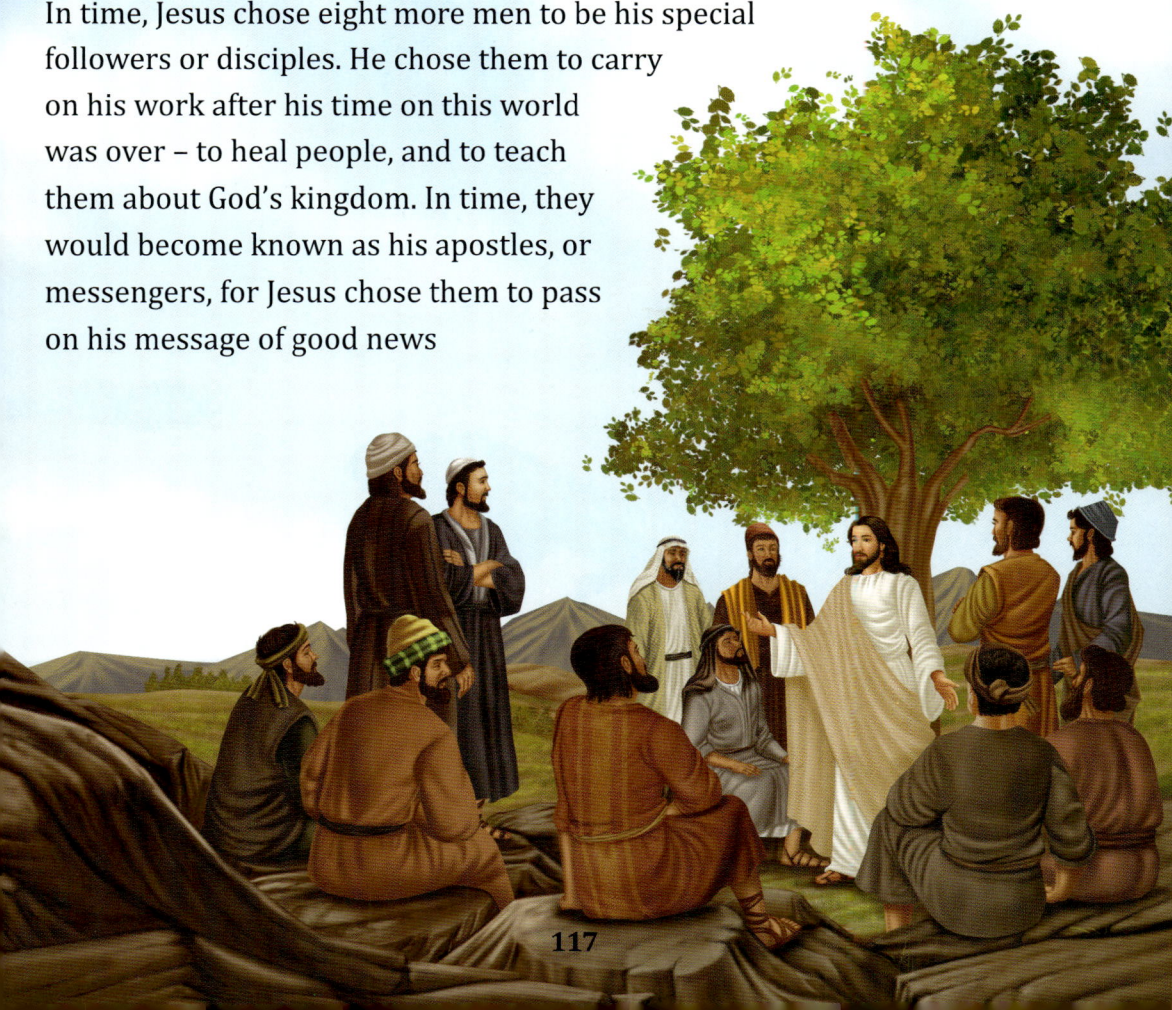

WATER INTO WINE

Jesus was invited to a marvellous wedding party along with his friends and his mother. Everything was going well until the wine ran out! Mary came to tell Jesus, who asked her, "Why are you telling me? It is not yet time for me to show myself." But Mary still hoped he would help, and spoke quietly to the servants, telling them to do whatever Jesus told them.

There were several huge water jars nearby. Jesus told the servants to fill them with water, and then pour the water into jugs and take it to the head waiter to

taste. When the head waiter tasted it, he exclaimed to the bridegroom, "Most people serve the best wine at the start of a meal, but you have saved the best till last!" for the jugs were now filled with delicious wine!

This was the first of many miracles which Jesus would perform.

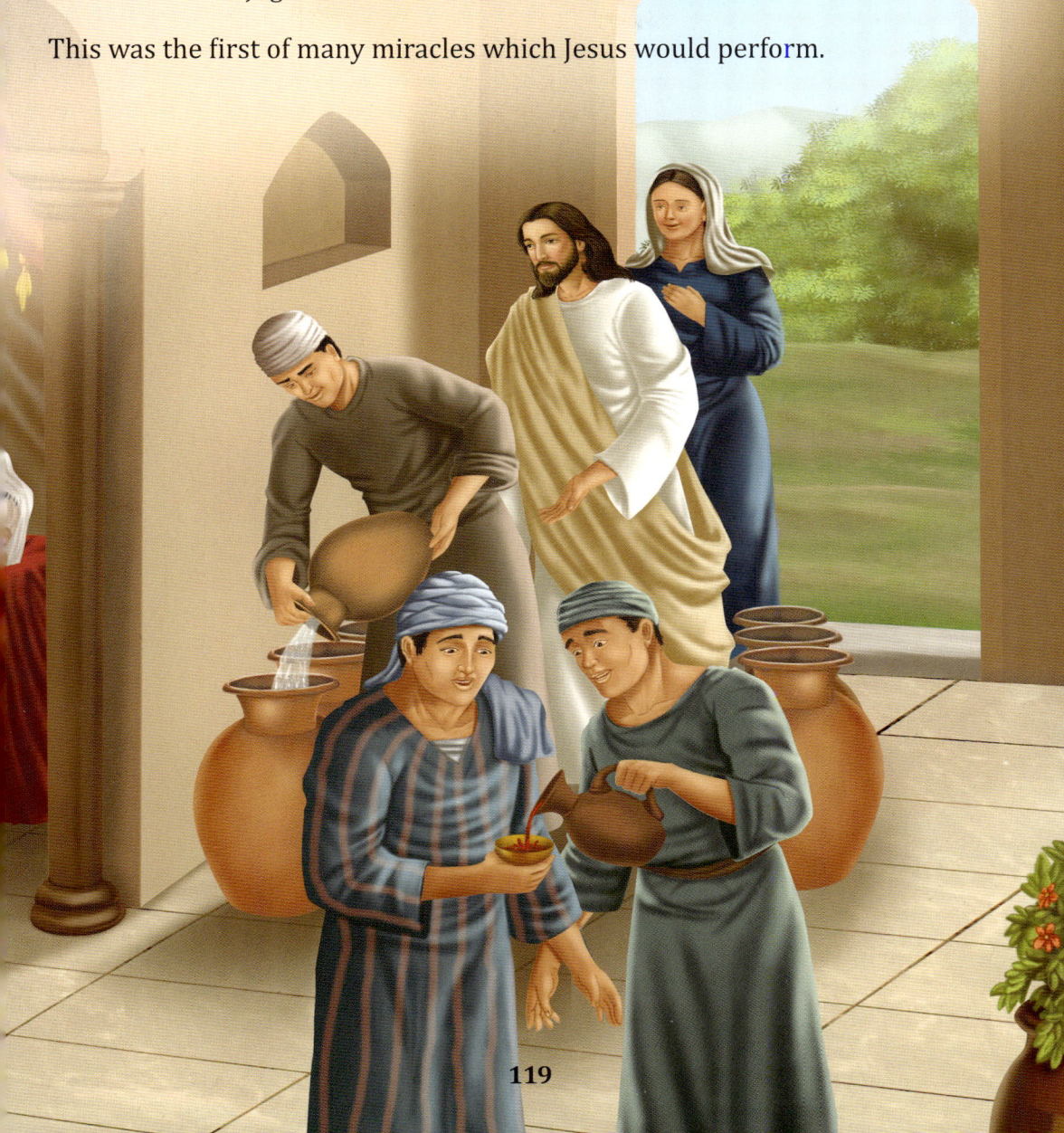

"YOU CAN MAKE ME CLEAN!"

One day, when Jesus went to the home of Andrew and Peter (who had been called Simon), Peter's mother-in-law was ill in bed with a fever. Jesus gently took her hand and helped her sit up. Instantly, she felt better. "I should be looking after you," she smiled at Jesus, and she jumped straight out of bed and began to get dinner ready for everyone!

News of her wonderful recovery spread like wildfire, and by evening a large crowd gathered outside – people who were sick or lame, blind or crippled, and others who were troubled by evil spirits. Many had brought friends or loved ones. They had all come to see if this amazing man could heal them, too. Jesus went out to them, and laying his hands on each one, he healed them.

One time, a man with leprosy, an awful skin disease, came up to Jesus and fell to his knees on the ground. "Sir, if you want to, you can make me clean," he begged humbly.

Filled with compassion, Jesus reached out to touch the man. "I do want to," he said. "Be clean!" and immediately the man's skin was perfectly smooth and healthy!

The grateful man simply couldn't keep the wonderful event to himself, and before long so many people wanted to come and see Jesus that he could no longer go anywhere without being surrounded by crowds.

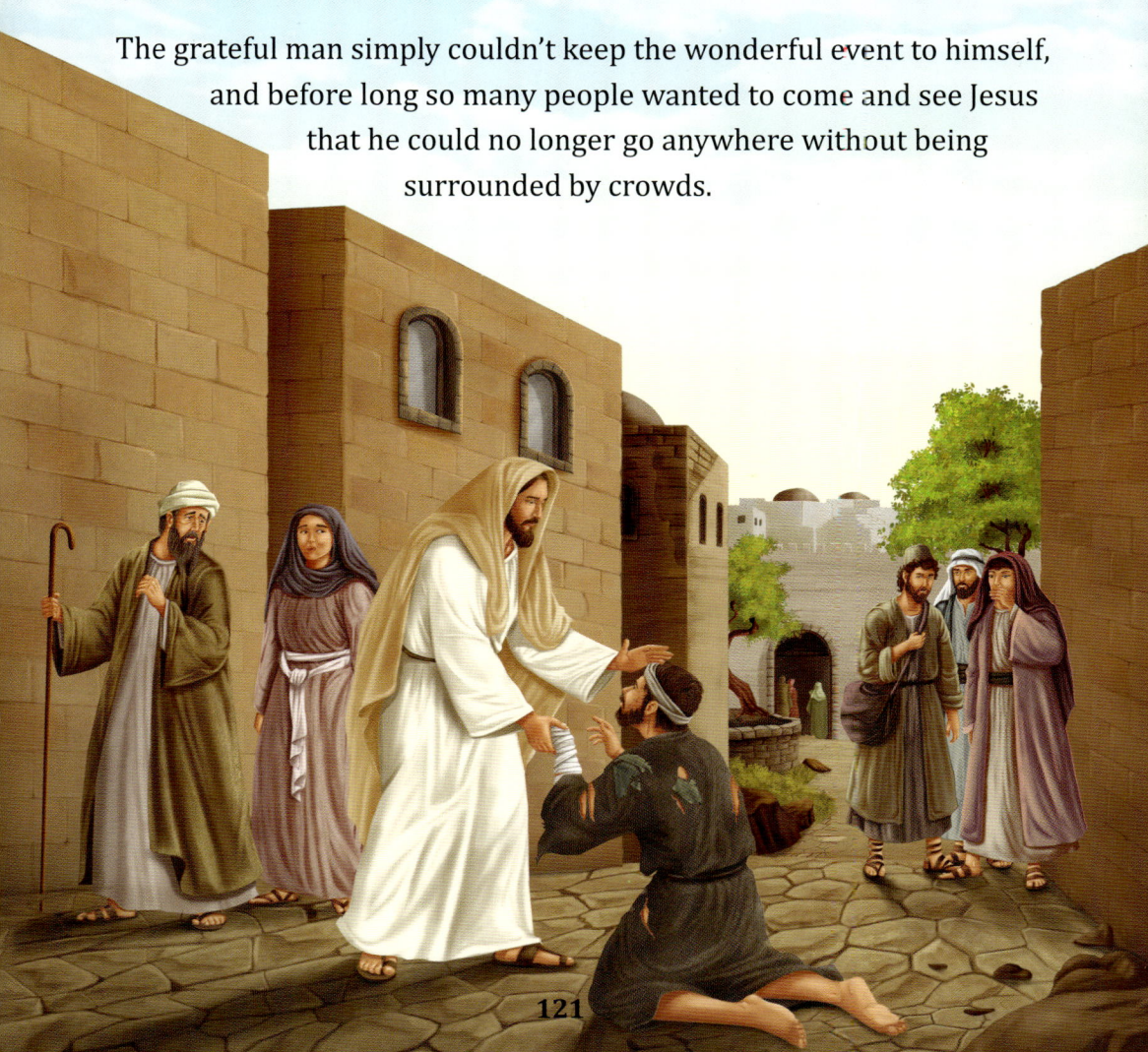

WHERE THERE'S A WILL ...

One time, some men brought their paralysed friend to be healed, but the house where Jesus was staying was so crowded they couldn't get in! Refusing to give up, they made a hole in the roof, and lowered the man down through it on a mat!

When Jesus saw how strongly they believed in him, he said to the man, "Your sins are forgiven, my friend."

This offended the teachers of the law, for only God could forgive sin. But Jesus said, "Is it easier to say to this man, 'Your sins are forgiven,' or to say,

'Get up and walk'? The Son of Man has authority on earth to forgive sins." Then he said to the man, "Get up, take your mat and go home." The man stood up, picked up the mat and walked out, and everyone was filled with wonder.

THE WOMAN AT THE WELL

Passing through Samaria, Jesus stopped at a well. When a woman came to get water, Jesus asked her for a drink. She was taken aback, because normally Jews wouldn't talk to Samaritans. She was even more surprised when he said, "If you knew what God can give you and who it is that asks, you would have asked and he would have given you living water."

The puzzled woman asked where he could get such water, and Jesus replied, "Those who drink this water will get thirsty again, but those who drink the water that I will give them will never be thirsty again."

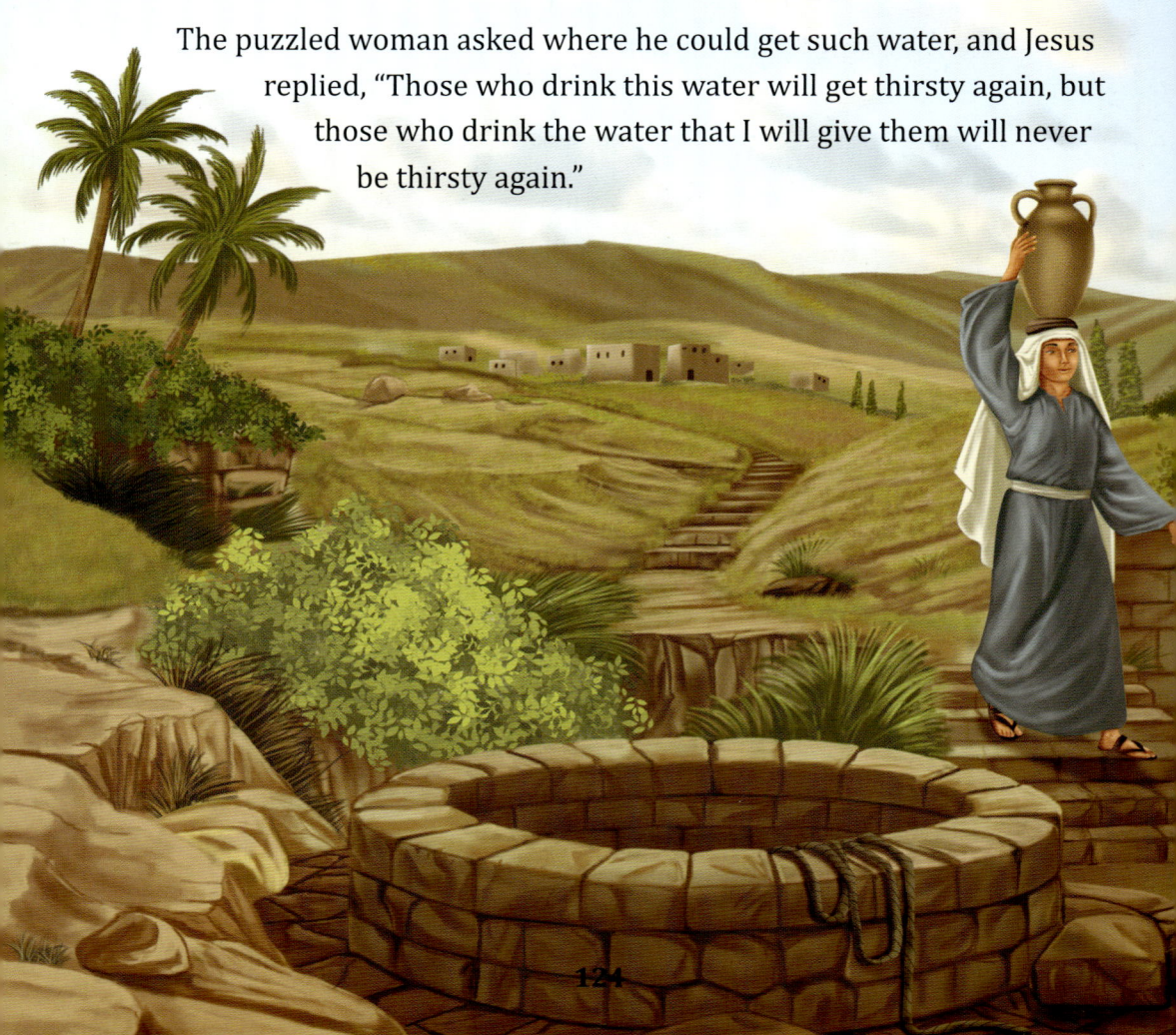

At this, the Samaritan woman asked eagerly, "Please give me this wonderful water!" But when Jesus told her to fetch her husband, she blushed and said she didn't have one.

Jesus said, "No, you have had five husbands, and aren't married to the man you are living with now."

The astonished woman ran to tell her friends about the amazing man who knew so much about her. "Do you think he could be God's promised king?" she asked. Many went to see him for themselves, and believed because of that day.

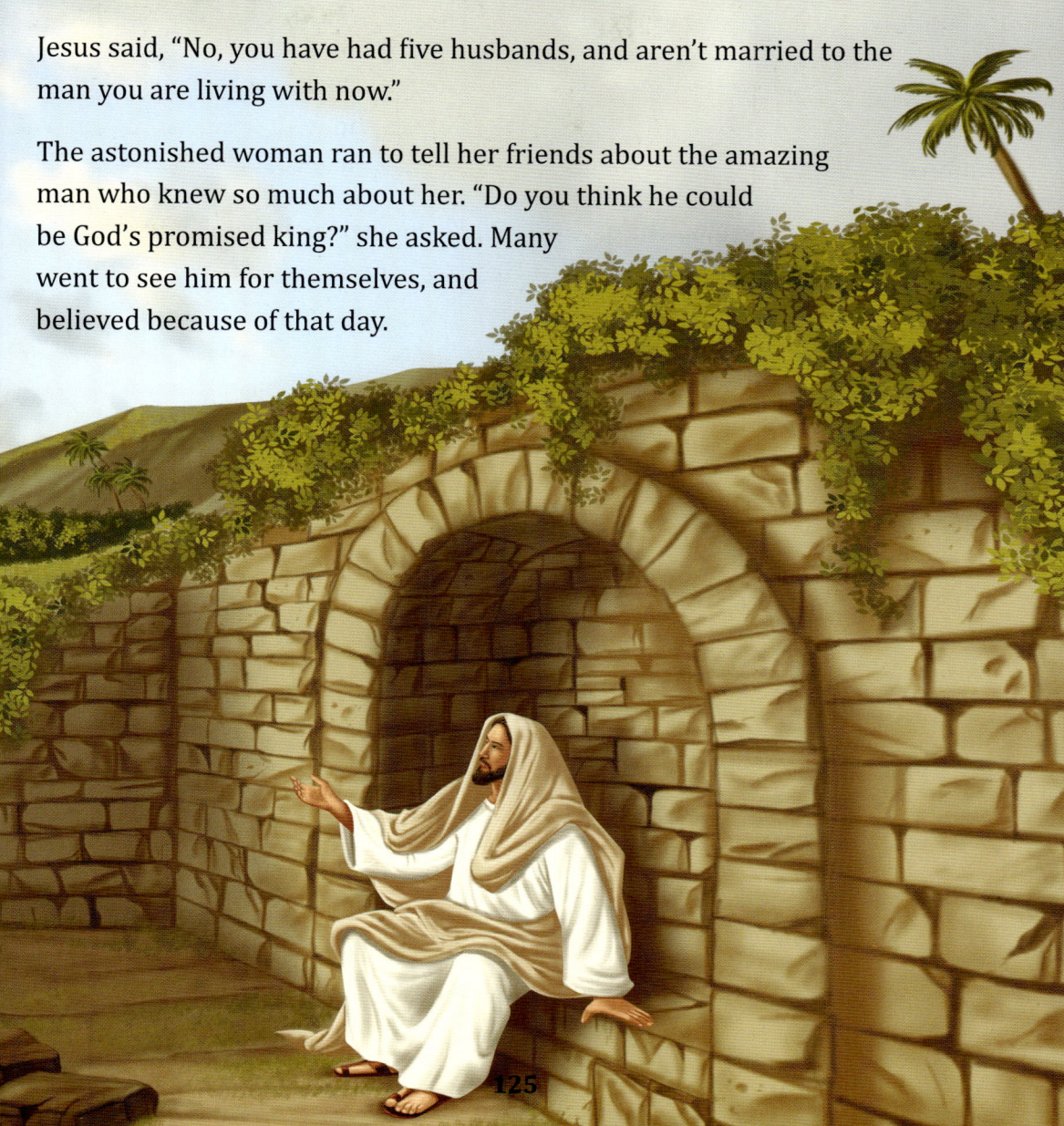

THE OFFICER'S SERVANT

In Capernaum there lived a Roman officer. Romans did not normally get on well with the Jews, but this officer was a good man, who treated the Jews well. He was also kind to the people in his household, but one of his servants was sick and close to death. When the officer heard that Jesus had come to Capernaum, he came to ask for his help.

Jesus asked him, "Shall I come and heal him?"

Then the officer replied, "Lord, I do not deserve to have you come to my own house, but I know that you don't need to in any case. If you just say the word, I know that my servant will be healed, just in the same way that when I order my soldiers to do something, then they do it!" The officer believed in Jesus so completely that he did not even need him to visit the sick man himself!

Jesus said to the crowd following him, "I tell you all, I have never found faith like this, even in Israel!"

And when the officer returned to his house, sure enough he found his servant up on his feet and feeling perfectly well again!

JUST SLEEPING

Jairus was desperate! His little girl was dreadfully ill, and he was worried that Jesus wouldn't be able to make his way through the crowds to heal her in time. Then Jesus stopped still and asked who had touched him. "Master, everyone is touching you in this crowd!" said a disciple, but Jesus knew that he had been touched in a special way.

As he looked around, a woman stepped forward and knelt at his feet. "Lord, it was me," she said nervously. For years she had been ill and nobody had been able to help her. But she had known that if she could just get close to Jesus, she would be healed, and truly, the moment she had touched the edge of his cloak, she was well!

Jesus wasn't angry. "Woman," he said to her kindly. "Your faith has healed you. Go home now." The woman was filled with gratitude, but at that very moment, someone came running up to say that Jairus's daughter was dead!

Jairus was heartbroken, but Jesus carried on walking. "Trust me, Jairus," he said. "Don't be afraid."

He arrived at the house to the sound of weeping. "Why are you carrying on so?" he asked. "The girl is not dead, she is just sleeping." The people there laughed at him, for they knew that the child was dead. Jesus ignored them and went to her room, where he took one of her hands in his own, and whispered, "Wake up, my child!"

In that instant, the child opened her eyes. She smiled at Jesus and hugged her overjoyed parents!

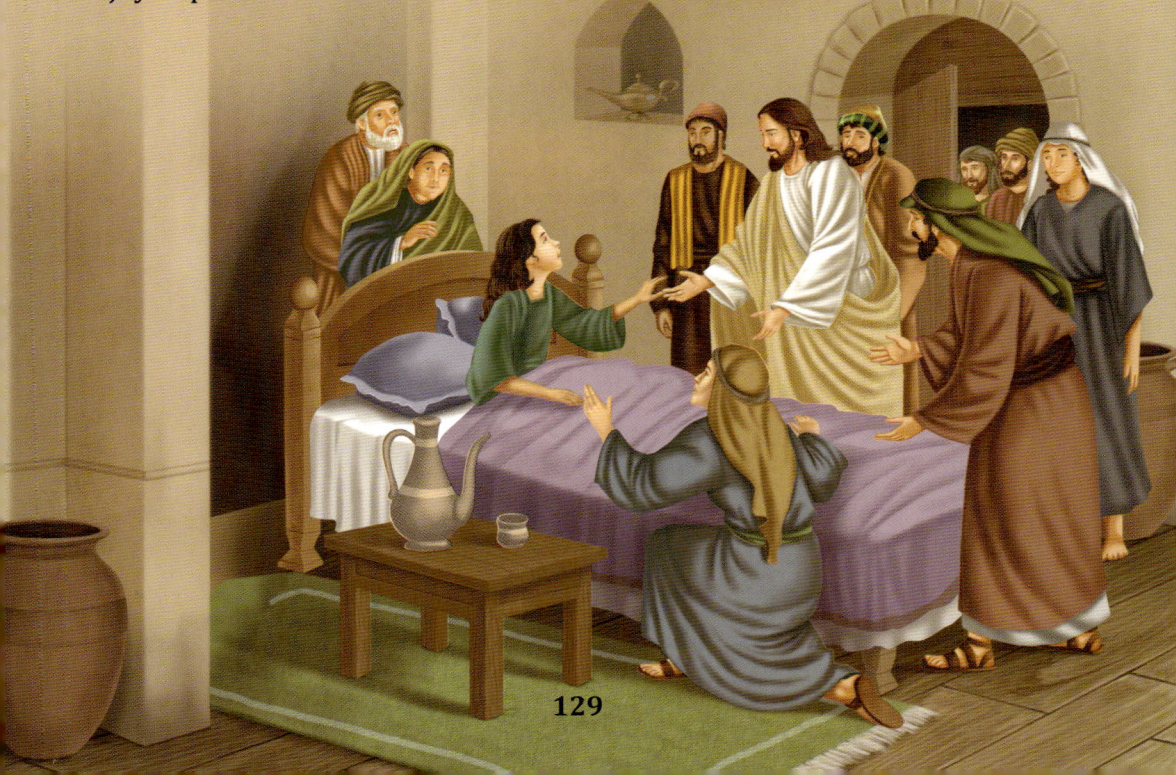

SERMON ON THE MOUNT

Jesus wasn't always welcome in the synagogues, so he would often teach his disciples and the crowds which gathered outside in the open air. One of the most important talks he gave was on a mountain near Capernaum. It has become known as the Sermon on the Mount. Jesus taught the people about what was truly important in life and gave comfort and advice:

"How happy are the poor and those who are sad or who have been badly treated, those who are humble, gentle and kind, and those who try to do the right thing – for all those people will be rewarded in heaven! They will be comforted and know great joy. Those who have been merciful will receive mercy, and God will look kindly on those who have tried to keep the peace, for they are truly his children. Be glad when people are mean to you and say nasty things about you because of me – for a great reward is waiting for you in heaven!"

Jesus went on, "It is important to obey all of God's laws, but you need to understand the meaning behind them. It isn't enough to not kill someone – you must learn to truly forgive to become close to God. So instead of thinking, 'An eye for an eye, and a tooth for a tooth,' if someone slaps you on the cheek, offer him the other one, too! Anger will eat you up. It's easy to love those who love you, but I say, love your enemies! God gives his sunlight and rain to both good and bad people!

"Treat others in the same way that you would like them to treat you. Don't judge them. Think about your own faults first!

"And let your life be an example to others, so that your light shines brightly, and all who see it praise God, too. But don't do good things just so people will look at you and think how good you are. You don't need their praise. Do your good deeds in private, and your Father, who sees everything, will reward you."

THE RIGHT WAY TO PRAY

Jesus told the people that they shouldn't spend their time trying to make themselves comfortable now. Instead, they needed to focus on the big picture. "Don't store up wealth on earth," he told them. "It won't last! Store up treasures in heaven, for where your treasures are, your heart will be too.

"And don't worry about what clothes you're wearing or where your next meal will come from. There is more to life than food and clothes. Look at the birds in the sky. They don't have to plant and harvest and store their food: God feeds them, just as he clothes the beautiful wild flowers. If God cares for the birds and the flowers, how much more does he love you?"

Jesus also taught people how to pray. They shouldn't try to impress others by praying in public, but should go to a quiet place and pray to God alone. Nor should they keep repeating meaningless words. God knows what is in our hearts, and this is the way Jesus told people to pray to him:

> *Our Father in heaven,*
> *Hallowed be your name.*
> *Your kingdom come.*
> *Your will be done,*
>   *on earth as it is in heaven.*
> *Give us today our daily bread,*
>   *and forgive us our sins,*
>   *as we forgive those who sin against us.*
> *Lead us not into temptation,*
>   *but deliver us from evil.*
> *For yours is the kingdom, the power,*
>   *and the glory, forever.*
>   *Amen.*

"Keep on asking," said Jesus, "and you will receive. Keep on seeking, and you will find. Keep on knocking, and the door will be opened to you."

A FIRM FOUNDATION

Before Jesus ended his sermon, he said one last thing: "If you listen to my teaching and follow it, then you are wise, like the person who builds his house on solid rock. Even if the rain pours down, the rivers flood, and the winds rage, the house won't collapse for it is built on solid rock. But he who listens and doesn't obey is foolish, like a person who builds a house on sand, without any foundations. The house is quickly built, but when the rains and

floods and winds come, the house will not be able to stand against them. It will collapse and be utterly destroyed."

As the crowds slowly dispersed, their heads were filled with all these new ideas. Jesus was nothing like their usual teachers, but what he said made sense. There was much to think about!

JESUS CALMS THE STORM

Jesus and his disciples climbed into a boat to travel across to the other side of the lake. Jesus was so tired that he lay down and fell asleep. Suddenly, the skies darkened, rain came pelting down, and a fierce storm struck the lake. Huge waves tossed the boat, and the disciples were terrified that they would capsize.

Jesus still lay sleeping. The frightened disciples went over and woke him up, begging him to save them. Jesus opened his eyes and looked up at them. "Why are you afraid? You have so little faith!" he said sadly. Then he stood up calmly, his arms spread wide, and facing into the wind and rain, commanded, "Be still!" At once, the wind and waves died down and all was calm.

The disciples were amazed. "Who is this man?" they asked themselves. "Even the winds and waves obey him!"

PARABLE OF THE SOWER

Many of the people who came to listen to Jesus were farmers. Jesus tried to pass on his message in a way that they would understand. His stories, often called parables, let people think things through for themselves. To some they would just be stories, but others would understand the real message.

"A farmer went out to sow his seed. As he was scattering it, some fell along the path and was trampled on, or eaten by birds. Some fell on rocky ground where there was no soil, and when they began to grow, the plants withered

because their roots could not reach water. Other seeds fell among weeds which choked them. Still others fell on good soil and grew into tall, strong plants and produced a crop far greater than what was sown."

Jesus was telling them that he was like the farmer, and the seeds were like the message he brought from God. The seeds that fell on the path and were eaten by birds are like those people who hear the good news but pay no attention. Those on the rocky ground are like people who receive the word with joy when they hear it, but they have no roots. They believe for a while, but when life gets difficult they give up easily. The seeds among weeds are like those who hear, but let themselves become choked by life's worries and pleasures. But the seeds that fell on good soil are like those people who hear God's message and hold it tight in their heart. Their faith grows and grows.

PARABLE OF THE WEEDS

Jesus told another parable: "Once a farmer sowed good seed in his field, but that night, his enemy sowed weeds among the wheat. When the wheat began to grow, weeds grew too. His servants asked if they should pull them up, but the owner said, 'If you pull the weeds up, you may pull some of the wheat up too at the same time. We must let both grow until harvest time. Then we will collect and burn the weeds, gather the wheat, and bring it into my barn.'"

Jesus later explained, "The farmer who sowed the good seed is the Son of Man. The field is the world, and the good seed is the people of the kingdom. The weeds were sown by the devil, and they are his people. The harvest will come at the end of time. Then the Son of Man will send out his angels, and they will weed out of his kingdom everything that causes sin and all who do evil and throw them into the blazing furnace, but the righteous will shine like the sun in the kingdom of their Father."

THE BIG PICNIC

His friends brought Jesus bad news about his cousin John – King Herod had ordered his execution. When Jesus heard, he tried to go somewhere quiet, but the people followed and he could not bring himself to send them away. When evening came, there was still a huge crowd. Jesus told his disciples to give them something to eat. "But Master," the disciples said, "there are thousands of people and we only have five loaves of bread and two fish!"

Jesus commanded them to tell the people to sit down. Then, taking the five loaves and the two fish and looking up to heaven, he gave thanks to his Father and broke the loaves into pieces. He gave them to the disciples, who took them to the people and then came back to Jesus for more bread and fish. He filled up their baskets again . . . and again . . . and again! To their astonishment there was still bread and fish left in the baskets when they came to feed the very last people! More than five thousand people had been fed that day – with five loaves of bread and two fish!

WALKING ON WATER

It was late at night and waves tossed the boat violently. Jesus had gone ashore to pray and the disciples were afraid. At dawn, they saw a figure walking towards them on the water! They thought it was a ghost and were scared until they heard the calm voice of Jesus, "It is I. Don't be afraid."

Peter was the first to speak. "Lord," he said, "if it is you, command me to walk across the water to you," and Jesus did so.

Peter put one foot gingerly in the water. Then he lowered the other, and bravely stood up, letting go of the boat. He didn't sink! But when he looked around at the waves, his courage failed him. As he began to sink, he cried, "Lord, save me!"

Jesus reached out and took his hand. "Oh, Peter," he said sadly, "where is your faith? Why did you doubt?"

Together they walked back to the boat. The wind died down and the water became calm. The disciples bowed low. "Truly you are the Son of God," they said humbly.

JESUS AND THE CHILDREN

Jesus loved little children, for they were good and innocent. He was always surrounded by children, and sometimes his disciples tried to shoo them away, thinking that they were bothering him.

"Don't stop little children from coming to me," he told them sternly. "The kingdom of heaven belongs to them and all those like them."

Once, when the disciples began arguing about which of them was the most important, Jesus beckoned to a little child and put his arm around her. He turned to his disciples, saying, "Whoever welcomes this child in my name welcomes me; and whoever welcomes me welcomes the one who sent me. For it is the one who is least among you who is the greatest. To enter heaven, you must be like a little child!"

THE GOOD SAMARITAN

Once someone asked Jesus what the Law meant when it said we must love our neighbours as much as ourselves. "Who is my neighbour?" he asked, and Jesus told him a story:

"A man was going from Jerusalem to Jericho, when he was attacked by robbers who beat him and took everything from him before leaving him by the roadside, half dead. Soon a priest passed by. When he saw the man, he crossed to the other side of the road and continued on his way. Then a Levite came along. He also hurried on his way without stopping.

"The next person to come along was a Samaritan, who are not friends of the Jews. Yet when this traveller saw the man lying bleeding by the roadside, his heart was filled with pity. He knelt beside him and carefully washed and bandaged his wounds, before taking him on his donkey to an inn, where he gave the innkeeper money to look after the man until he was well."

Jesus looked at the man who had posed the question, and asked who he thought had been a good neighbour to the injured man.

The man sheepishly replied, "The one who was kind to him."

Then Jesus told him, "Go, then, and be like him."

THE LOST SON

Jesus told another story to explain how happy God was when sinners returned to him: "There was once a man with two sons. The younger one asked for his share of the property so he could go out into the world, and he soon spent it all on enjoying himself. He ended up working for a farmer and was so hungry that sometimes he wished he could eat the food he was giving to the pigs! But at last he came to his senses and set off home to tell his father how sorry he was. "I'm not worthy of being his son," he thought, "but maybe he will let me work on the farm."

"When his father saw him coming, he rushed out and threw his arms around him. The young man tried to tell him that he was not fit to be called his son,

but the father told his servants to bring his finest robe for his son to wear and to kill the prize calf for a feast.

"The older son was outraged! He had worked hard for his father all this time, and nobody had ever held a feast for him! Yet here came his brother, having squandered all his money, and his father couldn't wait to kill the fattened calf and welcome him home!

"'My son,' the father said, 'you are always with me, and all I have is yours. But celebrate with me now, for your brother was dead to me and is alive again; he was lost and is found!'"

MARTHA AND MARY

Jesus was fond of two sisters, Mary and Martha. One day, he stopped to visit. Martha rushed off to make sure everything was clean and tidy and to prepare food, but Mary sat by his feet listening to all Jesus said.

Martha was angry. "Lord," she said to Jesus. "Won't you tell Mary to help me? She is sitting there doing nothing while I do all the work!"

"Martha," said Jesus in a soothing voice, "you are worrying about small things, but they're not what is really important. Your sister understands what is truly important, and it won't be taken away from her." He was trying to explain that the most important thing in life is to love Jesus and listen to his message!

Some time after this, Jesus received a message from Martha and Mary, telling him that their brother, Lazarus, was very ill. By the time Jesus arrived, Lazarus was dead. Martha wept, "Oh Lord, if you had been here, he would not have died. But God will give you whatever you ask."

Jesus said gently, "He will rise again. Everyone who believes in me will live again, even though he has died." But when Mary came up weeping, and he saw the other relatives crying, then Jesus wept, too, and asked to be taken to the cave where Lazarus had been laid. He told the men to open it.

Now, Lazarus had been dead for four days, but Jesus prayed and gave thanks to God. Then he said loudly, "Lazarus, come out!"

Everyone watched in silent wonder as a figure emerged from the dark cave, his hands and feet wrapped with strips of linen, and a cloth around his face. It was Lazarus, and he was alive!

THE RICH RULER

Once, a rich ruler came to ask Jesus what he must do to inherit eternal life. Jesus told him that he must keep all the commandments that Moses had been given, and the ruler replied, "All these I have kept since I was a boy."

Jesus looked at him. "You still lack one thing. Sell everything you have and give to the poor, and you will have treasure in heaven. Then come and follow me."

When he heard this, the ruler was sad, for he was very wealthy.

"How hard it is for the rich to enter the kingdom of God!" Jesus said. "In fact, it is easier for a camel to go through the eye of a needle than for someone who is rich to enter God's kingdom."

But to his disciples – who had left all they had to follow him – he said, "You can be sure that everyone who has left behind their home or their loved ones for my sake will be given so much more in return, as well as eternal life."

BE READY!

Jesus tried to make his followers understand that they must be ready at all times for his return, for they would never know when it might happen. He told them a story: "Once, ten girls were waiting to join a wedding feast. Five were foolish and brought no spare oil for their lamps. The other five were sensible, and brought extra oil. It was late, and the girls fell asleep, for the bridegroom was long in coming.

"Suddenly, at midnight, a cry rang out – the bridegroom was coming! Excitedly, the girls went to light their lamps, but those of the foolish girls began to flicker, for their oil had run out. They begged for more oil, but the wise girls replied, 'No,

there isn't enough for all of us. You must buy some more!' and they joined the bridegroom and went in with him to the feast.

"By the time the foolish girls returned with lighted lamps, the door was shut, and though they knocked loudly, they were told, 'You are too late. I don't know who you are!'"

Jesus told his disciples, "Always be ready, because you do not know the day or the hour of my return! When I do come, you must be ready. Just like the servants who have been left to look after their master's house when he is away, you must keep watch. For you do not know when the master will come back – it could be early in the morning, late at night, or anytime at all. Don't let him find you sleeping when he does return!"

ZACCHAEUS IN THE TREE

The streets of Jericho were lined with people eager to catch a glimpse of Jesus. Among them was a tax collector called Zacchaeus. Everyone hated tax collectors and believed that they stole some of the taxes to line their own pockets, so no one would make way for him, and he was too short to see over the crowd. He was feeling frustrated. Then he had a great idea – he would climb a tree! From its branches, he could see the procession as it made its way towards him. Perfect!

He almost fell off the branch when Jesus stopped right below, and said, "Zacchaeus, come down now. I must stay at your house today." Zacchaeus quickly scrambled down and bowed before Jesus, as the crowd muttered angrily about Jesus visiting a sinner!

But Zacchaeus was already a changed man. He said to Jesus, "Lord! I'm going to give half of everything I have to the poor, and if I have cheated anybody out of anything, I'll pay back four times the amount!"

Then Jesus turned to the crowd and said, "It is lost people like Zacchaeus that I came to save. Today he has found salvation!"

LOST AND FOUND

The Pharisees and the teachers of the law muttered amongst themselves when they saw Jesus mixing with tax collectors and sinners. Jesus explained how there will be far more rejoicing in heaven over the one sinner who repents than over the ninety-nine good people who don't need to!

Jesus asked them to imagine how a shepherd who had lost one of his flock would feel. Wouldn't the shepherd search high and low for the missing sheep, even though his other ninety-nine sheep were safe and sound? And how thrilled he'd be when he found the lost sheep, and how he would tell everyone about the precious sheep that had been found!

"The good shepherd," said Jesus, "would do anything for his sheep – even lay down his life to save them! He would never leave them!" Jesus was telling his listeners that he was like a shepherd, and that he would give up his life for each and every one of his flock!

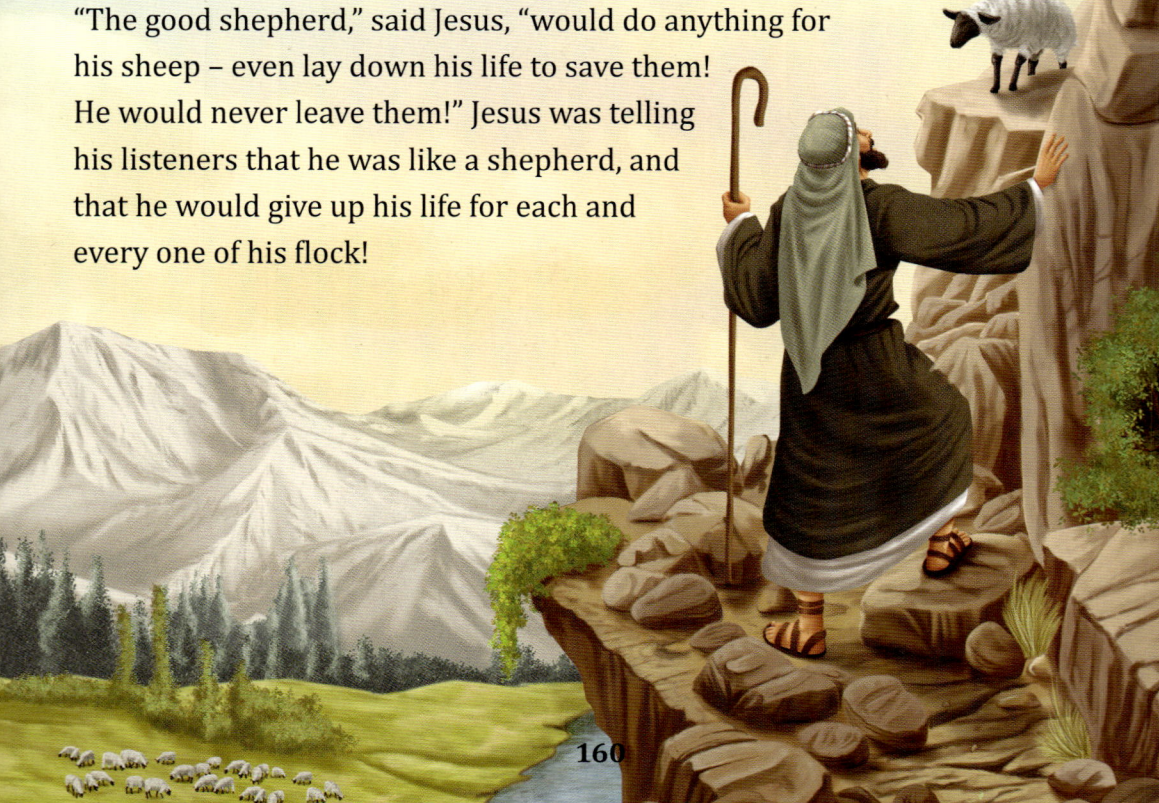

Then he told them to picture a woman who had ten silver coins and who had lost one of those coins. "Wouldn't she light a lamp?" Jesus asked them. "Don't you think she would take a brush, sweep every corner of the room, and search every nook and cranny until she found it? And when she did, how happy and relieved would she be? Surely she would get all her friends and neighbours together and tell them about the lost coin, and how she had found it, and ask them to be happy for her."

Jesus finished by saying, "In the same way, the angels will rejoice over every single sinner who repents."

Jesus cares about each and every one of us. He is never satisfied with all the people who do believe in him and try to live in the way he teaches. No, we are all so important to him that he will try to save every last one of us.

THE EXPENSIVE PERFUME

One evening, shortly before Passover, Jesus was dining with his disciples and friends in Bethany. Mary came to him, carrying an expensive jar of perfume. Kneeling before him, she carefully poured the perfume on his feet, using her own hair to wipe his feet. The house was filled with the wonderful fragrance.

Some started to scold her, for the perfume could have been sold to raise money for the poor. Jesus hushed them. "She has done a beautiful thing," he said. "You will always have the poor, and you can help them any time you want. But you won't always have me. People will remember Mary's kindness to me."

For Jesus would not be with them in this way for much longer. The final stage of his time on earth was about to begin.

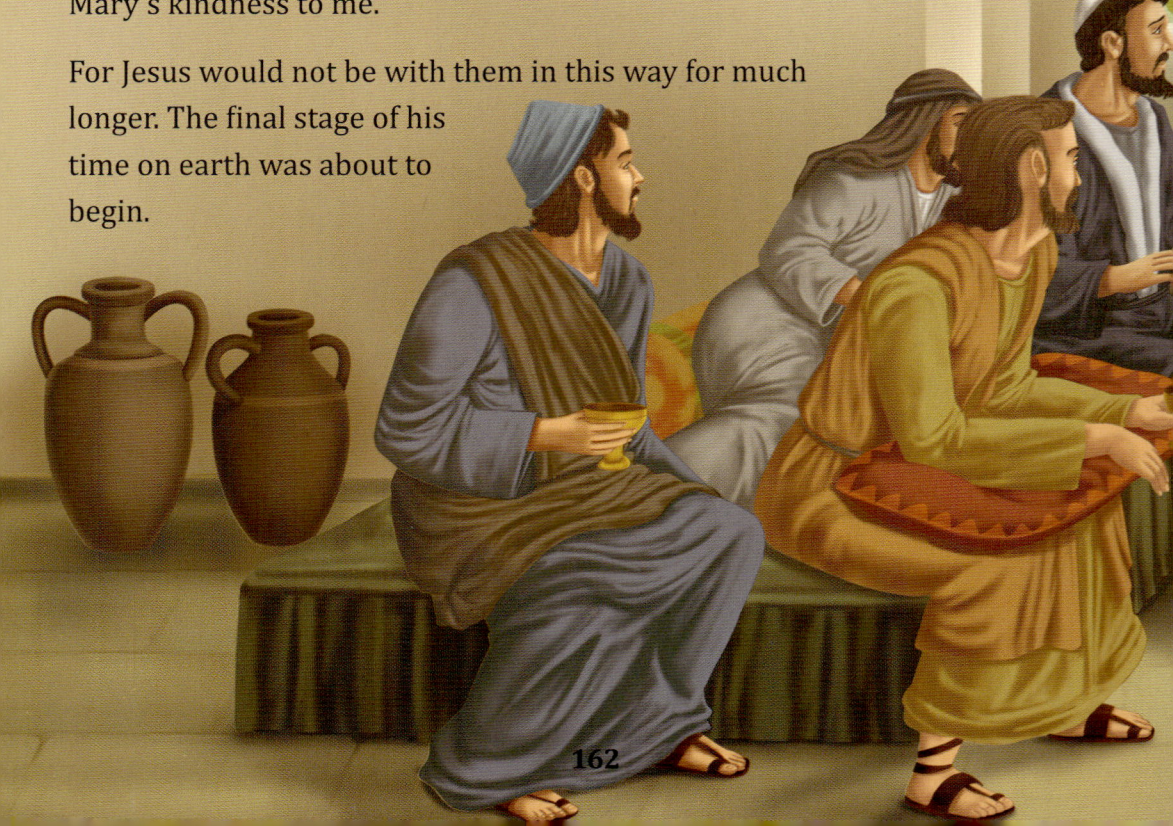

JESUS ENTERS JERUSALEM

Jerusalem was packed. It was the week of the Passover festival, and everyone had gathered to celebrate. It was also time for Jesus to start the last stage of his earthly life.

Jesus entered Jerusalem riding a humble donkey. Some of his followers threw their cloaks or large palm leaves on the dusty ground before him, and he was met by an enormous crowd, for many had heard of the miracles he had performed. The religious leaders might fear and hate Jesus, but many of the people truly saw him as their king, and they tried to give him a king's welcome.

His followers cried out, "Hosanna to the Son of David! Blessed is the king who comes in the name of the Lord!"

But Jesus was sad, for he knew that in a very short time these people cheering him would turn against him.

TROUBLE IN THE TEMPLE

The first thing Jesus did in Jerusalem was to visit his Father's temple. He was appalled to find that all the greedy, cheating people that he had thrown out before, were back again, trying to make money out of the poor people who came to make sacrifices to God.

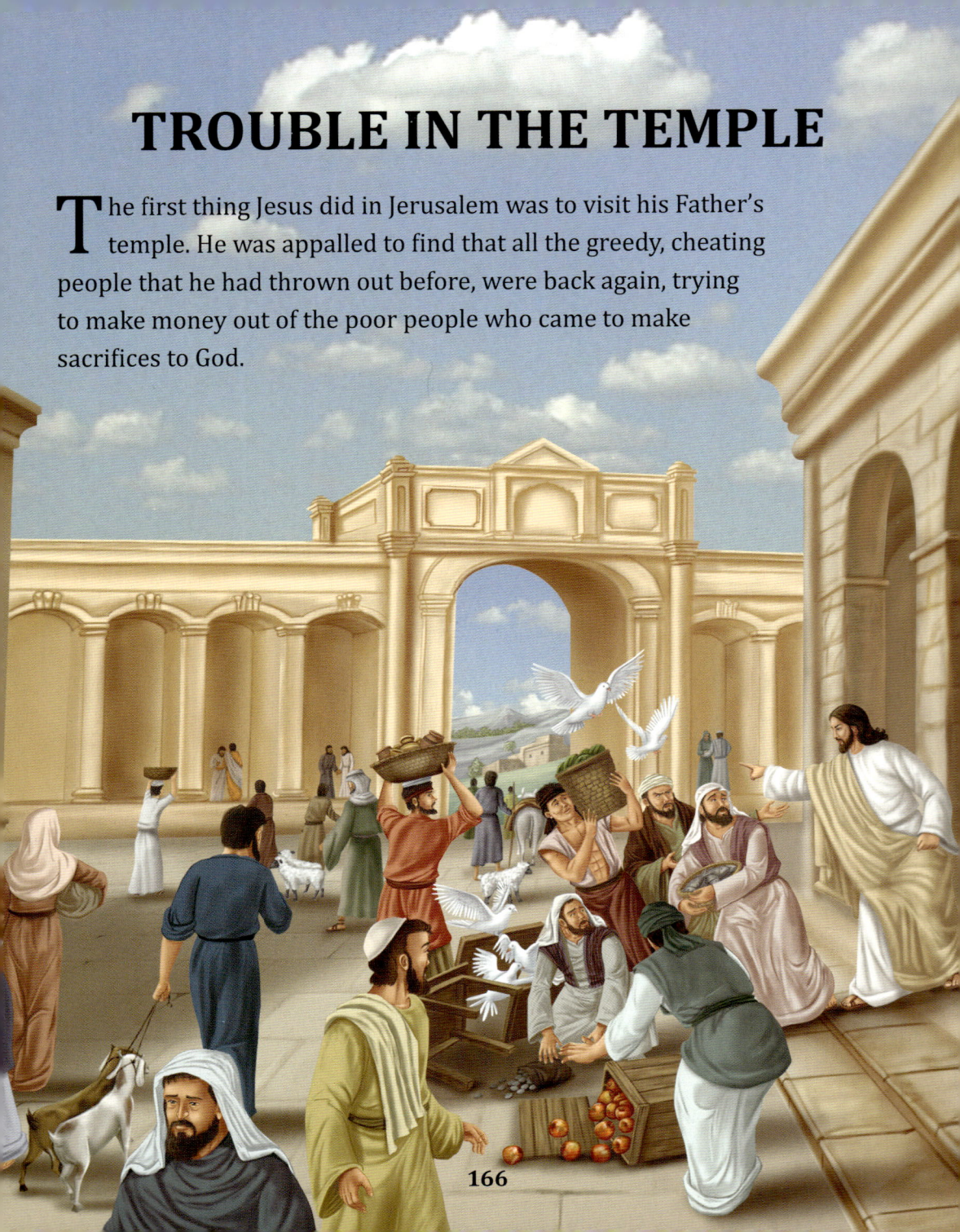

He looked around in anger, shouting, "No! God said that this temple was to be a place where people from all nations could come to pray to him. But you have made it a den of robbers!" and with these words he tore through the temple, throwing everyone out who shouldn't be there.

When he had finished and the temple was once again calm and tranquil, the poor people, the beggars and the sick began to find their way back in, and came to Jesus to be healed and to feel better. Children danced for joy around him, and everyone was happy – apart from the Pharisees, who plotted to get rid of him.

THE WIDOW'S OFFERING

Jesus was sitting in the temple, watching people put money in the collection boxes as offerings to God. Many rich people put in lots of clinking coins, making sure everybody knew how good they were being! Then along came a poor widow, her young children in threadbare clothes and bare feet. She put in two small copper coins. Together, they were worth less than a penny!

Jesus turned to his disciples. "Do you see that poor widow?" he asked. "The truth is, she gave far more than anyone else here today." The disciples looked puzzled. Surely her coins had been almost worthless!

Jesus tried to make them understand: "All those rich people had so much money that it was easy for them to give huge offerings – they still had plenty left. But that poor widow gave everything she had to give. She clearly loves God with all her heart, and trusts him to look after her, for she gave him everything she had."

LIKE A SERVANT

It was nearly time for the Passover feast, and a kind man had set aside a room for the disciples to prepare for it. That night, when they were eating, Jesus left the table, wrapped a towel around his waist, filled a basin with water and then, kneeling on the floor, began to wash and dry the disciples' feet like a servant.

The disciples were speechless, but when he knelt before Peter, the disciple protested, "Lord, you mustn't wash my feet!"

Jesus replied gently, "You do not understand what I am doing, but later it will be clear to you. Unless I wash you, you won't really belong to me," to which

Peter begged him to wash his hands and head too! But Jesus answered, "If you have bathed then you only need to wash your feet; your body is clean."

Jesus had washed their feet like a servant, so that they could learn to do the same for one another.

THE LORD'S SUPPER

Jesus knew he would soon have to leave his friends. "Soon, one of you will betray me," he said sadly. The disciples looked at one another in shock. Who could he possibly mean? They didn't know that Judas Iscariot, was dishonest and greedy, and had betrayed Jesus secretly to the Pharisees, promising to deliver him into their hands in exchange for thirty silver coins!

"The one who dips his bread with mine is the one," said Jesus, and when Judas dipped his bread into the same bowl, Jesus said softly, "Go and do what you have to do," and Judas left. But the others didn't understand.

Jesus handed around bread, saying "This is my body which will be broken." Next, he passed around a cup of wine, saying, "Drink this, it is my blood which will take away sin." Then he told them he would soon be leaving them.

Peter cried out, "But Lord, where are you going? Why can't I follow you? I would readily lay down my life for you!"

"And yet," said Jesus gently, "you will disown me three times before the cock crows!" Peter was horrified. He felt this could never happen!

Jesus told the disciples that he was going ahead to prepare a place for them in his Father's house, and that they would know how to find their way there. "I am the way and the truth and the life," he told them. "The only way to the Father is through believing in me. As the Father has loved me, so have I loved you. And I give you this command: love one another, just as I have loved each of you. There is no greater love than to lay down one's life for one's friends!"

A DARK NIGHT

Jesus and the disciples left the city to go to a quiet garden called Gethsemane. There, Jesus prayed to his Father. A crowd of people burst into the garden, many armed with weapons. At the head of them was Judas Iscariot. He had told the chief priests that he would kiss Jesus so that they would know whom to arrest, and as Judas approached him, Jesus said sadly, "Oh Judas, would you betray the Son of Man with a kiss?"

Peter struck out with his sword, but Jesus told him to put his sword away, and he allowed the soldiers to arrest him. "I am the one you have come to find," he said quietly. "Let these others go. You had no need to come here with swords and clubs."

When the disciples realised that Jesus was going to allow himself to be taken, they fled in fear and despair.

Peter followed the soldiers to the courtyard of the high priest, where he waited miserably, along with the guards warming themselves at the fire. A servant girl thought she recognised him, and asked if he was a follower of Jesus. Nervously, Peter told her she was mistaken, for he feared what would happen to him.

Later, the girl asked one of the guards if he didn't think Peter looked like one of Jesus' followers. Peter panicked and said he had nothing to do with Jesus, but now the other guards were looking at him. "You must be one of them," said one. "I can tell from your accent you're from Galilee."

"I swear I've never even met him!" cried Peter. At that moment, a cock crowed. Peter remembered what Jesus had said, and he wept in dismay.

PILATE WASHES HIS HANDS

The priests and Pharisees spent the night questioning Jesus. They were determined to find him guilty of something, for they hated and feared him. They dragged him before the Roman governor, Pontius Pilate, and demanded that he order his execution.

Pilate could find no reason to put Jesus to death. He offered the people a choice between sparing the life of either Jesus, or a murderer named Barabbas. The crowd chose Barabbas!

"What shall I do with the one you call King of the Jews?" Pilate asked.

"Crucify him!" roared the crowd, who had been stirred up by the priests.

Pilate did not want to order the execution – but neither did he want a riot! He sent for a bowl of water and washed his hands in it, to show that he took no responsibility for Jesus' death. Then he released Barabbas, and had Jesus handed over to be crucified.

Jesus was taken away by the soldiers, who mocked and beat him, before leading him through the streets towards Golgotha, the place where he was to be crucified.

They made him carry the wooden cross on his back, but it was large and heavy, and Jesus had been dreadfully beaten. When he could do it no longer, they snatched someone from out of the crowd to carry it for him. And so the dreadful procession made its way out of the city to the hill of Golgotha.

THE CRUCIFIXION

Soldiers nailed Jesus' hands and feet to the cross and placed above his head a sign saying, **'JESUS OF NAZARETH, KING OF THE JEWS'**. As they raised the cross, Jesus cried, "Father, forgive them! They don't know what they are doing."

Two thieves were crucified beside him. The first sneered at him, but the other said, "Be quiet! We deserve our punishment, but this man has done nothing wrong." Then he turned to Jesus and said, "Please remember me when you come into your kingdom," and Jesus promised he would be with him that day in Paradise.

At midday, a shadow passed across the sun and darkness fell over the land for three long hours. At three o'clock in the afternoon, Jesus cried out in a loud voice, "My God, why have you forsaken me?" Then he gave a great cry, "It is finished!" and with these words, he gave up his spirit.

At that moment the earth shook, and the curtain in the holy temple was torn from top to bottom. When the Roman soldiers felt the ground move beneath their feet and saw how Jesus passed away, they were deeply shaken. "Surely he was the Son of God!" whispered one in amazement.

ALIVE!

Early on the first day of the week, Mary Magdalene and some other women went to anoint Jesus' body, which had been placed in a sealed tomb and was watched over by guards. As the women came near to the tomb, the earth shook, the guards were thrown to the ground, and the women saw that the stone had been rolled away from the entrance. Inside the tomb, shining brighter than the sun, was an angel!

The terrified women fell to their knees, but the angel said, "Why are you looking for the living among the dead? He is not here – he has risen just as he said he would!" The women hurried away to tell the disciples the news, afraid yet filled with joy.

Later that day, Mary Magdalene stood sadly outside the tomb. Some of the disciples had come and had since left, in wonder and confusion. Mary Magdalene was alone now. She heard steps behind her, and a man asked, "Woman, why are you crying? Who are you looking for?"

Thinking this must be the gardener, she begged, "Sir, if you have moved him, please tell me where he is, and I will get him." In reply, the man only spoke her name, but instantly she spun around. She recognised that voice!

"Teacher!" she gasped, and reached out towards Jesus. He told her to go and tell the others what she had seen, and so Mary rushed off with the amazing news that she had seen Jesus alive!

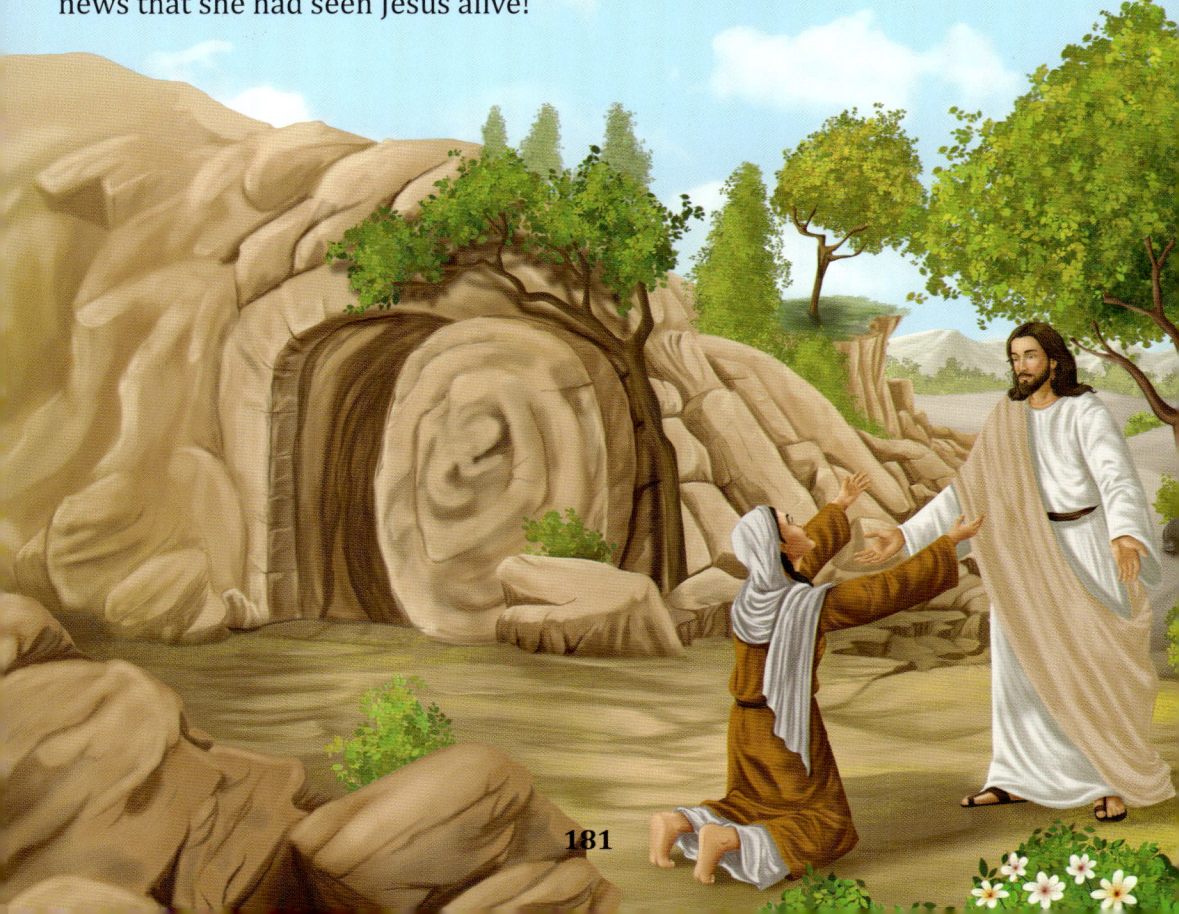

A STRANGER ON THE ROAD

That same day, two of Jesus' followers were travelling along the dusty road from Jerusalem to a village. They couldn't stop talking about the last couple of days. Soon, another man approached them and asked what they were talking about.

"Where have you been?" they asked in amazement, and went on to tell him excitedly all about Jesus, the amazing things he'd taught, and the miracles he'd performed. Then, more sombrely, they told of his death and his disappearance from the tomb.

"How slow you are to believe what the prophets told you!" said the stranger. "Don't you see that the Messiah had to suffer these things and then enter his glory?" and he began to talk to them about everything that had been said in the Scriptures about Jesus. They were enthralled, for he made everything so clear.

At the village, they urged him to dine with them. As they were eating, he took some bread and, giving thanks for it, broke it into pieces and handed it to them. Suddenly, they realised who this stranger really was – Jesus himself! And then he vanished!

The friends hurried back to Jerusalem. They couldn't wait to tell the disciples the good news.

DOUBTING THOMAS

That same evening, Jesus appeared to the disciples. At first, they couldn't believe it. Was he a ghost? But he spoke to them, reassuring them, and showing them his hands and feet with their scars. "Touch me and see," he said. "A ghost does not have flesh and bones!" Then he went on to explain the Scriptures to them, and they were filled with joy and wonder.

Now, Thomas was not with the others, and when they tried to tell him about it, he couldn't believe them. "Unless I put my finger where the nails were, and touch the wound in his side, I will not believe," he said stubbornly.

A week later, Thomas was with the disciples when suddenly, Jesus was among them again. Turning to Thomas he said, "Put your finger in the wounds in my hands. Reach out and feel my side. Stop doubting and believe!"

Thomas fell to his knees, overcome with joy. Now he believed!

Jesus said, "You only believed because you saw me yourself. How blessed will people be who believe without even seeing!"

THE ASCENSION

Jesus and his friends were on a hillside outside Jerusalem. The time had come for Jesus to leave the world. In the time since his resurrection, he had made many things clearer to them, and had told them a little about what the future would hold.

Jesus turned to his disciples. "You must stay here in Jerusalem for now, and wait for the gift that my Father has promised you, for soon you will be baptised with the Holy Spirit. Then you must spread my message not only in Jerusalem and Judah and Samaria, but in every country!"

He held up his hands to bless them and then, before their eyes, he was taken up to heaven, and a cloud hid him from sight.

As they stood looking upwards in wonder, suddenly two men dressed in white stood beside them. "Why are you looking at the sky? Jesus has been taken from you into heaven, but he will come back again in the same way that he left!"

THE HOLY SPIRIT

It was ten days since Jesus had been taken up to heaven. The twelve disciples (for they had chosen a man named Matthias to join them to take the place of Judas Iscariot) were gathered together when suddenly the house was filled with the sound of a mighty wind coming from heaven.

As they watched in wonder, tongues of fire seemed to rest on each person there. They were all filled with the Holy Spirit, and began to speak in different languages – languages they had never spoken before or studied!

Hearing the commotion, a huge crowd gathered outside. They were amazed when the disciples came out and began talking in different languages! "How can this be?" they exclaimed. "There are people here from Asia and Egypt, from Rome and Arabia – how are we all hearing them using our own languages to tell us about God?"

Peter stepped forward. "Listen!" he said. "We have been filled with the Holy Spirit! A few weeks ago, Jesus from Nazareth died on a cross. Yet God has raised Jesus to life! This was all God's plan. Jesus was sent to you by God, but you rejected him, and had him killed by evil men. But death could not hold him! God made Jesus Lord and Messiah!"

The people looked worried and upset. What had they done? And how could they make it better?

"If you really are sorry," Peter went on, "then repent. Be baptised in the name of Jesus Christ. Your sins will be forgiven and you will receive the gift of the Holy Spirit. This promise is not just for those of you who are here today – God's gift is for everyone, everywhere!"

TROUBLE!

A man sat begging outside the temple gates. He was lame and spent every day there, hoping for a spare coin or two. Now, as Peter and John passed by he looked up hopefully.

Peter stopped. "I don't have any money," he said. "But I can give you something far better! In the name of Jesus Christ, I order you to get up and walk!" and to everyone's astonishment, he helped the lame man to stand up. The man tried a few cautious steps, and then a few more, and then walked straight into the temple to give thanks to God!

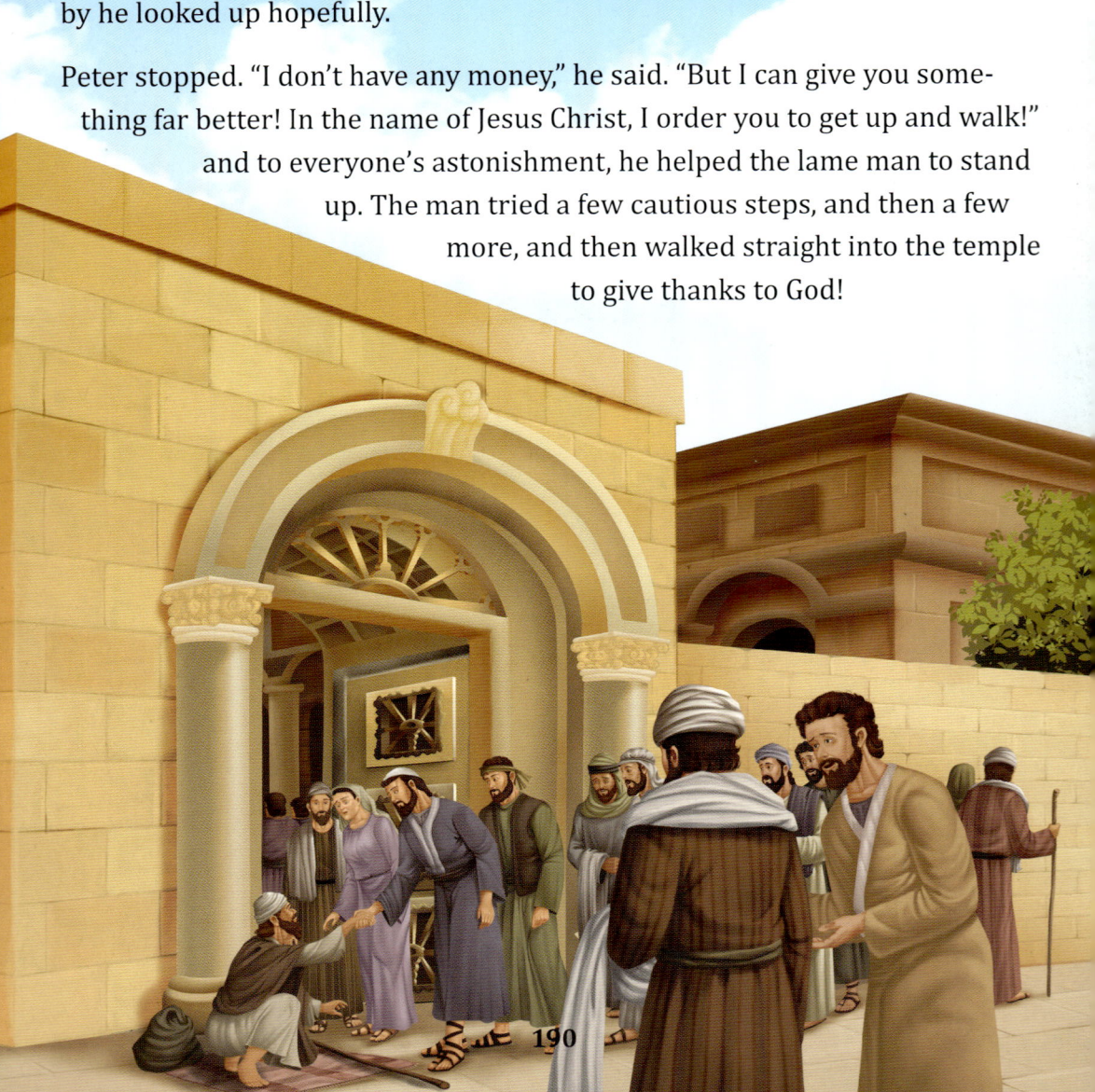

When the Jewish leaders heard, they threw Peter and John into prison – they wanted people to listen to *them* – not the apostles! But during the night, an angel opened the doors of the jail and brought them out, telling them to go back to the temple courts and spread their message.

The priests sent for them the next morning, only to find the jail locked but the cell empty! When the apostles were found and brought before them, the priests accused them of disobeying their instructions. But Peter and the others bravely replied, "We must obey God rather than human beings!"

In the end, the apostles were released under strict instructions not to talk about Jesus any more – but of course they did!

PHILIP AND THE ETHIOPIAN

Philip was one of the apostles of Jesus. He preached to many people, not just Jews. One day, an angel called him to travel south from Jerusalem. As he was travelling, Philip came across a powerful and wealthy man – the treasurer to the queen of Ethiopia – who was reading from the Book of Isaiah as he travelled in his fine carriage.

The Ethiopian was frustrated – he was reading Isaiah's words about how God's servant was led like a sheep to the slaughter, and wanted to know whom the prophet was talking about. Philip explained that it was written about Jesus, and went on to tell him all about God's Son.

The official wanted to become a Christian right away, and so Philip baptised him in a river by the roadside! God took Philip away to preach the gospel in many other places, but the Ethiopian carried on his way, filled with joy and happiness.

SAUL SEES THE LIGHT

Saul was an enemy of the Christians. He wanted to put a stop to their preaching, and believed he was doing God's will. Many Christians had fled to the city of Damascus, so he set off after them. Suddenly, a blinding light from heaven flashed down. Saul fell to the ground, covering his eyes. Then he heard a voice say, "Saul, why do you keep on persecuting me?"

Saul began trembling. He asked who was speaking, though he really knew.

"I am Jesus," replied the voice. "Get up and go into the city, and you will be told what you must do."

Saul struggled to his feet, but when he opened his eyes, he couldn't see a thing! His guards led him into the city where he fasted for three days, spending his time in prayer.

God had great plans for Saul. He sent a Christian named Ananias to him, and when he touched Saul, it was as if scales fell from his eyes and Saul could see once more! He arose and was baptised.

Saul (or Paul – for he became known by the Roman version of his name) began to spread the good news about Jesus in Damascus. People were amazed, for he had once been the fiercest enemy of the Christians, yet he went on to become one of the greatest of all the apostles!

THE SHEET OF ANIMALS

One day, while praying on the roof under the hot sun, Peter fell asleep and had a strange dream. In his dream, there hung before him a huge white sheet being lowered from heaven by its corners. It was filled with all sorts of animals, reptiles and birds. Looking closely, he realised they were all creatures that Jews were forbidden to eat, for they were considered 'unclean.' Then he heard God's voice saying, "Get up, Peter. Kill and eat."

"Surely not, Lord!" Peter cried. "I have never eaten anything unclean!"

The voice spoke again, "Do not call impure what God has made clean."

This happened three times, then the sheet was pulled back up to heaven.

Peter awoke to the sound of knocking. Downstairs were three men sent by an officer named Cornelius. Although they were Romans, Cornelius and his family believed in God. God had told Cornelius to have Peter brought to his house. The men were

Gentiles (that is, they were not Jews), but Peter invited them in, for now he understood his vision, and the very next day he went with them to Cornelius' house, where his friends and family had gathered.

Peter looked around. These people were Gentiles but they were all ready to listen to what he had to say about Jesus. "God doesn't show favouritism," Peter told them. "He will welcome anyone who believes in him and tries to follow his laws."

While he was talking about Jesus, the Holy Spirit came. God had given the Gentiles the same gift that he had given to Jesus' special disciples. God's message is for all the people of the world, not just for Jews. That is what Peter's vision had meant!

SINGING IN PRISON

God sent Paul on a journey to spread the good news to people who hadn't yet heard about Jesus. He travelled to many places with different companions, going from town to town, preaching the good news. If the Jews wouldn't listen, they taught the Gentiles. They made many friends – and many enemies! Once, when travelling in Macedonia, he and his companion, Silas, were thrown into prison.

It was midnight. Paul and Silas were lying in the stocks. The chains were tight and the wood heavy, but they did not despair. Instead, they prayed and sang hymns. The other prisoners could hardly believe their ears!

Suddenly, an earthquake shook the prison, the cell doors flew open, and everyone's chains came loose! The terrified jailer was about to kill himself, fearing punishment, but Paul called out, "Don't harm yourself! We're still here!"

The astonished man took Paul and Silas to his own house, where he and his family spent the night learning about Jesus. They became Christians that very night!

Paul and Silas returned to the prison. When officials came the next morning, Paul told them they were Roman citizens

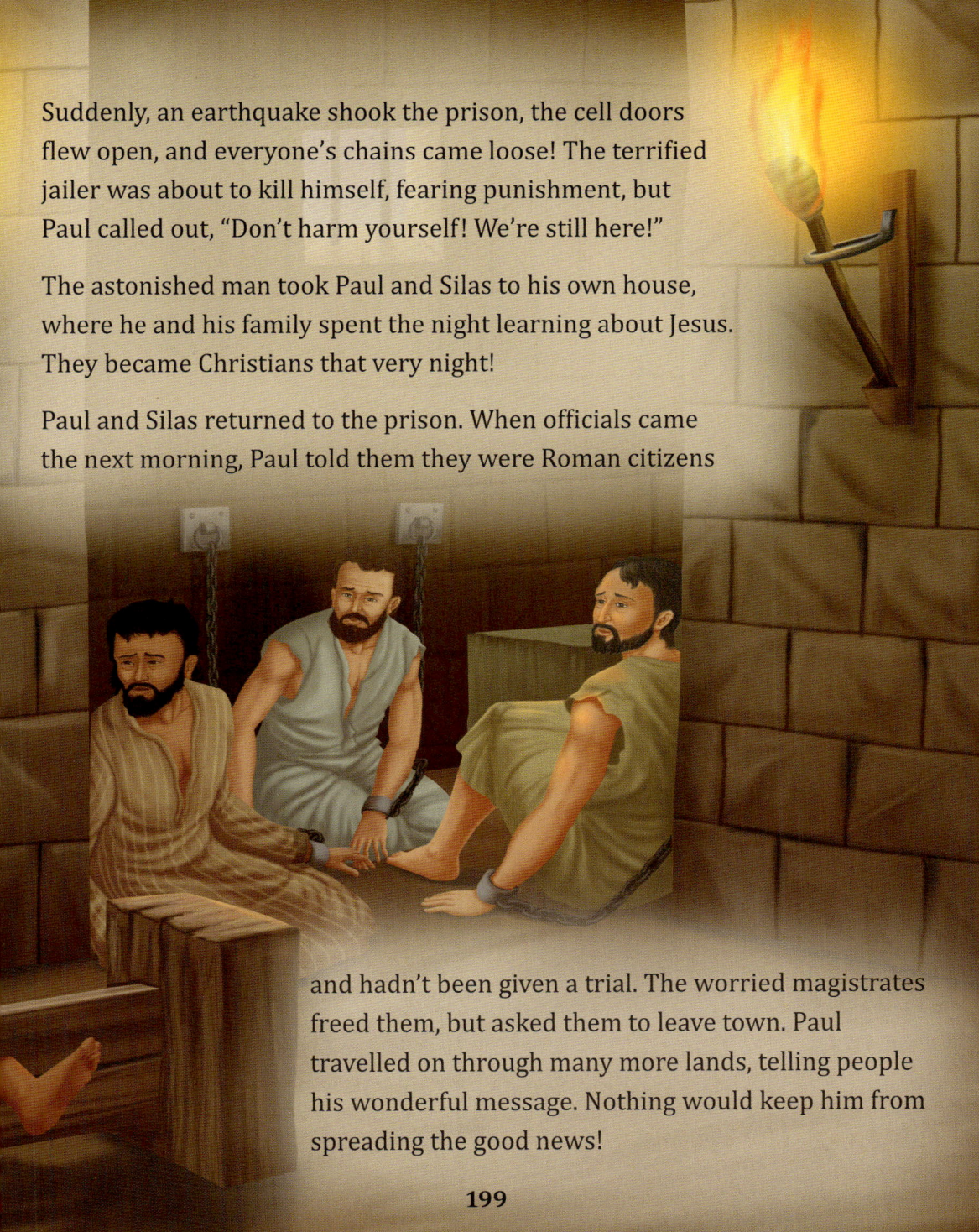

and hadn't been given a trial. The worried magistrates freed them, but asked them to leave town. Paul travelled on through many more lands, telling people his wonderful message. Nothing would keep him from spreading the good news!

STORM AT SEA

Paul was on board a ship, heading for Rome. He had returned to Jerusalem to do God's work, and his enemies had imprisoned him. Now he was on his way to have his case heard by the emperor himself, but the journey was beset with delays and bad weather. Paul knew that it wasn't safe to continue, but the captain ignored him and soon they found themselves in the middle of a dreadful storm. For days, the ship was at the mercy of the angry sea, and all hope seemed lost.

Paul spoke to the crew and passengers to comfort them. He told them an angel had promised they would all reach land safely, but they needed to trust in God. After two whole weeks, the coastline finally came into sight!

Suddenly, the ship struck a sandbar, and began to be broken to pieces by the surf! The soldiers planned to kill the prisoners to prevent any from escaping, but the centurion in charge ordered everyone who could swim to make for land, and told those who could not swim to cling to the wreckage and float ashore. In this way, every last person reached land safely, just as God had promised!

Paul and his companions found themselves on the island of Malta. They were cold and wet, but they were alive! Some islanders came to help. They lit a fire to warm them. While Paul was putting some extra wood on the fire, a poisonous snake slithered out and fastened itself on his hand. Paul calmly shook the snake off and carried on as if nothing had happened. The astonished islanders thought he must be a god!

After three months, they set sail once again for Rome. While he waited for his case to be heard, Paul was allowed to live by himself, with a soldier to guard him. Although he was not allowed out, he could have visitors, and so was able to carry on spreading the message to new people. He also wrote letters to the Christians he had met during his travels, to encourage and help them as they set up their churches.

THE GREATEST OF THESE

Paul wrote to the people in the new churches, to strengthen them in their faith, and to allay their doubts and fears. "I believe that our present suffering is not worth comparing with the glory that will be revealed in us – and suffering itself produces perseverance, and so character and hope! Nothing will ever be able to separate us from the love of God which is ours through Christ Jesus our Lord – not hardship, or persecution, or hunger, or poverty, or danger, or death."

He encouraged them to live good lives, filled with love and kindness: "Love must be sincere. Hate what is evil; cling to what is good. Share what you have with those in need."

He reminded them that they owed the gifts they had – whether they could speak in foreign languages, or prophesise, or teach, or heal – to the Holy Spirit. They must not get big-headed, but must work together.

"Unless you feel love for people," he wrote to them, "all the good things you do are meaningless. Love is patient and kind. It isn't jealous, boastful, selfish, proud or rude. It is steady and true, and it never, ever gives up. Three things will last forever – faith, hope, and love – and the greatest of these is love."

Paul kept faith in the Lord until the very end of his days!

"I'M COMING SOON!"

The very last book of the Bible is Revelation. Many believe it was written by the disciple John. The author had an amazing vision in which he saw that a terrible time will come when all will be judged, but those who are faithful to Jesus will be protected by the seal of God. Dreadful things will happen to the earth, but finally all that is evil will be destroyed and God's Kingdom will reign. After the Final Judgement, a new heaven and earth will replace the old.

John wrote: "Then I saw a new heaven and earth, and I saw the Holy City coming down out of heaven like a beautiful bride. I heard a loud voice speaking from the throne: 'Now God's home is with his people! He will live with them. They shall be his people, and he will be their God. There will be no more death, no more grief, or crying, or pain. He will make all things new! For he is the first and the last, the beginning and the end.'

"And I was shown the Holy City, shining with the glory of God. Its temple is the Lord God Almighty and the Lamb. The city has no need of the sun or the moon, because the glory of God shines on it, and the Lamb is its lamp. The people of the world will walk by its light, and the gates will never be closed, because there will be no night there. But only those whose names are written in the Lamb's Book of Life will enter.

"'Listen!' says Jesus. 'I'm coming soon!'"

Let it be so! Come, Lord Jesus, come soon!